*To Joseph,
Sorry, messed up the spelling!
Congrats on your graduation
and everything you do!*
*Pam Acena
aka
Rose
Cerona*

The Ancient

Paths

Rose Cerona

(Also available in an 8.5 x 8.5)

Acknowledgements

It is with a much love and gratitude that I would like to give honor to and remember my mother who told me before she passed away that I needed to get this book published. This story is a part of her life too.

I would like to thank the many people who believed in this story before it became published, including Larry Neidert the love of my life, my friend Holley Roberts, Mary Crutcher, Diane Nelson, my sister Carol and my friend Julia Hartman.

I am fortunate to have friends such as Jasmine Parks and Connie Malone who have prayed with me so many times that it is impossible to keep track. Our friendship has been like a three-strong cord which is not easily broken. Michaelle McGinnis has been key to helping me survive times of extreme doubt and times of feeling shaken to the core as I struggled to make sense of the battles I was going through. Kimra Steckbeck has been a voice of reason and has lent a willing ear and helped to birth this book by having the title ready on the tip of her tongue when I was so uncertain of which way to go with that decision.

I would like to acknowledge and give thanks to my publisher, Theresa Nichols for accepting this story and believing even in the face of naysayers. She had the vision and saw what God intended this book to be. And last but not least, I thank Jasmine Parks for guiding me to Theresa. Without Jasmine, this story may never have gotten told.

The Ancient Paths

Thus says the Lord,

Stand at the crossroads, and look,

And ask for the ancient paths,

where the good way lies; and walk in it,

And find rest for your souls.

But they said, "We will not give heed."

(Jeremiah 6:16)

Prologue

How does one even begin to tell when darkness has entered their life? How do you describe darkness—how do you recognize the face of evil when it comes? And how do you find your way back from the hellish, hallowed halls of darkness once you realize you have entered that unintended dimension?

The lives of the family living deep within of the hollows of Hickman County, Tennessee would forever be altered because of a fateful visit from a stranger who would appear, as if out of the recesses of one's imagination. The lives of four young children would one day be tragically derailed from their intended course, in particular, one young girl named Rose. Would she be able to find her way back?

The Ancient Paths

List of Characters by Alphabetical Order

Agent Fielding	FBI agent
Alana	Edwina's youngest daughter
Anna	Rose's middle sister
Arlo	Wealthy, platonic (for awhile) friend of Rose
Barky	Mrs. Barrett's pet Chihuahua
Belladonna	Tosha's doll
Bo	older brother to Edgar and Alex/Rose's new boyfriend
Clarence	Husband of Emma/Rose's step-grandfather
Cousin Joe	Emma's cousin/second cousin to Margie and Leroy
Dabney and Tim	Hippie couple who Rose meets through Don and Marianne
Daniel	Pet dog to Rose and her siblings
Deborah	Woman with prophetic gifting
Don and Marianne	Hippie neighbors of Rose and her family
Edgar and Alex	Fraternal twins/friends of both Tony and Rose/Rose's classmates
Edwina	Jose's girlfriend
Elizabeth	Daughter of Mr. and Mrs. Davis
Emma	Mother of Margie/Rose's grandmother

The Ancient Paths

Gerald	Edwina's son
Greg	Rose's high school sweetheart
Harvey	Jose's boss
Howie	Rose's childhood friend
Jay	Lil's boyfriend
Jeanine	Nursery worker at the gym
Jeff and Randy	Classmates of Rose's/Jeff would be very significant to Rose
Jessica	Daughter of Don and Marianne
Joel	Geeky classmate of Rose's
John	Tony's friend from school
Jose	Margie's husband/ Rose's father
Judge	Divorce judge
Karen	Rose's sister
Kelly	Edwina's oldest daughter
Kevin	A foster child/ward of the Barrett's
Larry	Manager at bar where Rose works
Laurie	Rose's best friend in high school
Leroy	Brother of Margie/Rose's uncle
Lil	Rose's Aunt/Margie's younger sister
Little girl	Possessed child at the gym
Lorraine	Rose's oldest aunt

The Ancient Paths

Lydia	Bo's other girlfriend that he cheats on Rose
Margie	Mother of main character Rose
Maria	Arlo's friend/Jeweler
Mark and Thea	Son and daughter of Mr. and Mrs. Caldwell
Miz Minnie	Elderly woman, neighbor, and Rose's childhood friend
Mr. & Mrs. Barrett	Foster parents to Rose, Tony, Anna and Karen
Mr. & Mrs. Caldwell	Neighbors of Rose and her family
Mr. Benson	Margie's divorce attorney
Mr. Butts	Mrs. Barrett's pet baboon
Mr. Davis/George	Co-worker of Jose's
Mrs. Davis/Miriam	Mr. Davis' wife
Mrs. Kraus	Social worker
Mrs. Silva	English teacher
Nick	Margie's new Greek husband/ Rose's new stepfather
Roger Zimmerman	Wealthy businessman and Jose's new boss
Roland	Gorgeous stranger at party/ significant character in Rose's life
Rose	Main character
Samuel Peters	Private Investigator

Scott	Tony's friend who is at Centennial Park
Sharon	Edwina's middle daughter
Sherry	Live-in nanny to Rose, Tony, Anna and Karen
Sue	Tosha's mother
The Caravan	A commune of hippies who moved to Nashville from California
Tony	Rose's older brother
Torie	Greg's secret flame
Tosha	Tony's girlfriend/Rose's antagonist
Two questionable characters	Men in a car who give Rose and Anna a ride
Willie	Rose's childhood friend

List of characters

(Other than Rose, all characters are listed in order of appearance in the story)

Rose	Main character
Margie	Mother of main character Rose
Leroy	Brother of Margie/Rose's uncle
Emma	Mother of Margie/Rose's grandmother

The Ancient Paths

Clarence	Husband of Emma/Rose's step-grandfather
Cousin Joe	Emma's cousin/second cousin to Margie and Leroy
Jose	Margie's husband/ Rose's father
Judge	Divorce judge
Tony	Rose's older brother
Anna	Rose's middle sister
Karen	Rose's sister
Mr. Benson	Margie's divorce attorney
Edwina	Jose's girlfriend
Kelly	Edwina's oldest daughter
Sharon	Edwina's middle daughter
Alana	Edwina's youngest daughter
Gerald	Edwina's son
Howie	Rose's childhood friend
Willie	Rose's childhood friend
Miz Minnie	Elderly woman, neighbor, and Rose's childhood friend
Harvey	Jose's boss
Roger Zimmerman	Wealthy businessman and Jose's new boss
Mrs. Kraus	Social worker
Mr. & Mrs. Barrett	Foster parents to Rose, Tony, Anna and Karen
Kevin	A foster child/ward of the Barrett's
Barky	Mrs. Barrett's pet Chihuahua
Mr. Butts	Mrs. Barrett's pet baboon
Sherry	Live-in nanny to Rose, Tony, Anna and Karen
Mr. & Mrs. Caldwell	Neighbors of Rose and her family
Mark and Thea	Son and daughter of Mr. and Mrs. Caldwell

Mr. Davis/George	Co-worker of Jose's
Mrs. Davis/Miriam	Mr. Davis' wife
Elizabeth	Daughter of Mr. and Mrs. Davis
Daniel	Pet dog to Rose and her siblings
John	Tony's friend from school
Samuel Peters	Private Investigator
Lil	Rose's Aunt/Margie's younger sister
Jay	Lil's boyfriend
Nick	Margie's new Greek husband/Rose's new stepfather
Greg	Rose's high school sweetheart
Joel	Geeky classmate of Rose's
Mrs. Silva	English teacher
Laurie	Rose's best friend in high school
Scott	Tony's friend who is at Centennial Park
Edgar and Alex	Fraternal twins/friends of both Tony and Rose/Rose's classmates
Jeff and Randy	Classmates of Rose's/Jeff would be very significant to Rose
Bo	older brother to Edgar and Alex/Rose's new boyfriend
Don and Marianne	Hippie neighbors of Rose and her family
Jessica	Daughter of Don and Marianne
Dabney and Tim	Hippie couple who Rose meets through Don and Marianne
The Caravan	A commune of hippies who moved to Nashville from California
Torie	Greg's secret flame

The Ancient Paths

Lydia	Bo's other girlfriend that he cheats on Rose with
Tosha	Tony's girlfriend/Rose's antagonist
Belladonna	Tosha's doll
Arlo	Wealthy, platonic (for awhile) friend of Rose
Maria	Arlo's friend/Jeweler
Sue	Tosha's mother
Roland	Gorgeous stranger at party/significant character in Rose's life
Lorraine	Rose's oldest aunt
Agent Fielding	FBI agent
Two questionable Characters	Men in a car who give Rose and Anna a ride
Larry	Manager at bar where Rose works
Deborah	Woman with prophetic gifting
Jeanine	Nursery worker at the gym
Little girl	Possessed child at the gym

Part 1

CHAPTER 1

As the red and white 1952 Studebaker sped through the sluggish, hot, hazy and humid back roads of Hickman County, it sent gravels spewing in every direction and clouds of dirt flying as it hummed along with its radio blaring out the sounds of Hank Williams' music. Beside the road stood a dirty, sweaty old farmer in overalls who had stopped for a dip of snuff and a water break. He spat out the tobacco as the Studebaker roared past him and left him literally eating dirt as the dust swirled about his face. "Darned old city folks, get a job!" he yelled, raising his fist in the air in a motion of defiance at the car as it sped on.

In a place like Hickman County, Tennessee, not much ever seemed to change. It was one of those places where time seemed to literally stand still. With its clear, clean springs flowing through the area, this part of the county had been given the name Bon Aqua which was French for 'good water.' Usually, not many strangers ever made their way back into the hollows of the county; however, this was one day which would prove not to be quite so usual.

And on this day, somewhere deep within the hollows of Hickman

County was an old country home, where the cool, sparkling creek separated the front yard from the graveled dirt road. A thick strip of metal was placed over the very narrow body of running water so that folks could come and go over the creek without getting their feet wet. The front and side yards of the home were huge, and there was plenty of space between the big green house and the neighbors.

Margie, who was a seventeen-year-old enchanting, burgeoning country flower with curly, auburn hair and hazel green eyes, and her brother Leroy who was eighteen, opened the screen door of their mother's family homestead and stepped onto the front porch. Margie's elongated, slender body spoke of her country girl innocence, as well as the transformation of changing from a child to a woman. The siblings were now part of the third generation to live in the old home.

Margie carried two glasses of ice tea in her hands. Leroy seemed barely able to put one foot in front of the other. Each step was an effort. Margie placed the glasses of tea onto the wooden floor boards of the front porch then turned toward her brother. "Okay, Buddy, easy does it," she said, as she gently but firmly held her brother's arm and helped him lower himself into his seat.

Leroy was a couple of years older than Margie, but because her big brother had been born with muscular dystrophy, Margie had always made it a point to help take care of her older brother. "Thanks, Sis. Don't know what I'd do without ya, girl."

14

"Now tell me something I *don't* know," she smirked, as she handed Leroy his glass of tea and playfully thumped him on the head. A moment after she had seated herself comfortably on the top porch step, Margie was greeted with a sobering splash of cold ice tea against the back of her head. "What the…" She whirled around, noted the look of innocence on her brother's face, and pointed her index finger at Leroy to scold him.

"What's the matter, sis? Just thought I'd help you cool off a little bit," Leroy smirked. Margie gritted her teeth as she cut her beautiful hazel eyes at him. But, even she had to laugh at herself, because she knew she had deserved that. Leroy picked up his acoustic guitar, which sat in the chair beside him, and strummed a few chords. "Hmm, looks like somebody's already been out here pickin' this morning," he mused.

As Margie lounged on the top step of the porch tapping her foot in time to the twangs of the guitar, the heat of the afternoon raged on, the melodious tinkling sound of the creek softly permeated the air, the crickets joined the song of nature, and Leroy and Margie sang a song he had written: "How can I ever let you know, that my love has begun to grow. Only a year or two ago it seems, all of these things were only my dreams. I gaze into your eyes, and I can see you are very wise. Believe me my dear, it's oh so true. Without you, my world would be so blue. No past or present can compare to the heaven on earth that you and I share."

15

Leroy stopped abruptly and ran his fingers through his thick head of hair. He was already tired. "I'm sorry, sis. I know I haven't been out here long, but it's just too darn hot. Would you mind, please?" He reached his arm toward her for help. Like the adoring younger sister that she was, Margie stood beside her brother and lovingly placed one hand on his forehead and one hand on his shoulder. "All right then, Buddy. One, two, three and up we go!" And with that, she helped him to pull himself into an upright position from his chair.

"Thanks, Sis. I...I don't know what I'd do..."

She grinned at her brother and said gently, "Aw. Now, tell me something I don't know."

The sound of car brakes screeching to a grinding halt caught their attention, and they both jerked their heads toward the direction of the road. There weren't too many cars other than their own family car and that of the only neighbor who lived beyond them that made it this far down into the hollow. The Studebaker had come to a stop on the road by the creek in front of their home. The radio was still blaring, but quickly faded into a dead silence once the car engine was turned off.

As Margie and Leroy looked on, Cousin Joe who was a bit older than them, since he was actually their mother's cousin, stepped out from behind the steering wheel and waved a big hello. Leroy propped his right elbow with his left hand and waved. Under his breath, Leroy murmured, "Ooh wee. Wait'll mama sees this." Then his voice grew louder, and he yelled across the yard so that Joe would hear him on the other side of the creek, "Uh, howdy Joe! How are ya, cuz?"

Then it happened. Margie's whole world stopped when out from the passenger side of the vehicle stepped the most incredibly, honest to goodness, semi-tall, dark and handsome man she had ever laid eyes on her in her life! There was something so different about him, something almost dark and sinister about the way he looked, and yet so penetratingly beautiful. As Margie watched in a trance-like state, he walked with such grace and ease that he seemed to glide over the small bridge that lead him into the yard. Margie placed her hand over her heart and tapped her chest, "Be still my achin' heart. There *is* a God."

Leroy overheard her and whispered in her ear, "Shut up, sis! You know you're just dreamin. Besides, that fella's old enough…he's old enough…to be your uncle. You're still a baby." It was true. Margie was only sixteen and this man was thirty-two, twice her age.

But, she was not discouraged. "I can assure you, Bubba, I'm not dreamin'. I'm wide awake," she responded dreamily.

"Well, you might be awake, but you're still a mess with that ice tea in your hair," he chuckled.

The Ancient Paths

While Cousin Joe and the dark stranger climbed the steps up to the porch, Margie continued staring holes through the stranger. She was just a young teenager and had never seen many people who looked quite as different as he did.

"Hey, Leroy, Margie, where's your Ma? This here is Jose…Jose Rivera. Say hello to the nice folks, Jose."

Leroy looked in the direction of the front door and yelled, "Mama! Cousin Joe is here, him and his…friend!"

Emma sailed through the front door wiping her hands on her faded floral apron and swatting at the lock of hair hanging down in her eyes, and her husband Clarence followed on her heels. She threw her arms around her cousin's neck and had to choke back tears. "Darn, Joe. How long has it been anyway, about seven or eight years now? Where the heck have you been?"

Joe jokingly whispered, "You could have done so much better than Clarence. What kind of name is that anyway?"

"Shut up, you moron," Emma laughed as she smacked him on the head. That seemed to be the accepted token of affection for this family, a hefty whack on the noggin.

Over Joe's shoulder, Emma's eyes slowly came to rest on the figure of the stranger who had arrived at her home with her cousin. A look of recognition slowly found its way into her eyes as they narrowed and focused squarely on Jose. She knew she had seen that face somewhere before…but, where?

Jose took Margie's hand and shook it, "I am so glad to make your acquaintance." Margie was so mesmerized by his presence she could only stare some more. She was awestruck. She had never been exposed to anyone beyond the boundaries of Hickman County. It was sheer fascination she had upon meeting this dark, handsome stranger. She had never, ever, seen anything quite like him. She knew he was a bit older than her, but that didn't matter. He was someone new and different, and she was spell bound. In addition, at the age of sixteen, Margie was young, naïve, and gullible.

Looking at Margie, Cousin Joe explained, "This here is Jose. He used to be married to your cousin, Rachel."

"So, you're not a cousin, but you were married to a cousin? I haven't seen Rachel since we were little bitty things. Well, it's a pleasure to make your acquaintance, Jose." Her southern brogue was to die for, he thought. He just loved the way she said, "Jose."

Two weeks later, with Margie's family—including Emma, Clarence, Margie's cousins, aunts, uncles, brothers and sisters present,

The Ancient Paths

Margie and Jose were married in her mother's living room. Only, Jose had no family present at the wedding. So, where were they?

CHAPTER 2

Jose stood in the judge's chamber counting out ten one hundred dollar bills. The exchange between Jose and the judge was almost a whispered hush. "See that it happens," Jose grimaced.

"This never took place today," the judge retorted, counting the money, then pocketing it.

"Good, because I have no idea what you are referring to," Jose came back flippantly. He stepped out of the judge's office, looked quickly in both directions and disappeared into the men's room.

Moments later, Emma and Clarence were in the courtroom, seated with Tony, Rose, Anna and Karen, the four children born to Jose and Margie. They ranged in age from nine to four, Tony being the oldest, Rose next, then Anna and, last but not least, Karen. Rose, who was now seven years old, was escorted by the bailiff to the witness stand. "Sit down here, young lady." Rose looked scared to death, but she climbed onto the chair and sat looking wide eyed and terrified of the judge and the entire proceeding.

Without wasting a moment, the judge moved immediately into

questioning the young girl. "Rose, do you want to live with your daddy?" he asked. Rose was mortified. How could she know what to say, when she loved her mother terribly, had never seen her dad that much, but at the same time was scared of what her father would do if she said "no"? How did a child who had only had brief snippets of her life with her father in between his trips overseas and back answer such a question?

She started to cry, "Yes," she blurted. The pressure was too much for her young mind to take. She took one look at her father and she caved, and for the life of her, she could not figure out why she had just said "yes" when her heart was saying "no." It was a move on her part that she would live to regret for many years.

"Okay, you can step down young lady," the judge addressed Rose in a somewhat softer manner.

Margie turned to her attorney, Mr. Benson, "That's just not right! My kids are too young to be put on the witness stand and made to answer such a difficult question in front of everyone!" She knew from the expression on Rose's face that she had answered out of fear.

"I agree," her attorney consented, "but there is nothing I can do to stop this now."

Next, Tony was brought to the witness stand. "Young man, do you

22

want to live with your father?" the judge bellowed.

Tony was visibly shaken. No one but the judge could see his young hands wringing together in his lap. "Uh...I guess so, sir," was all Tony could manage to force out of his mouth, his voice barely audible.

"My gosh! Somebody stop this, please!" Margie insisted to Mr. Benson.

Mr. Benson stood, "Objection, your Honor."

"Sit down, Counselor!" the judge roared. "Objection overruled. Besides, I am through anyway. You may step down young man." Tony was obviously nervous and shaken from being made to choose one parent over another. What child wouldn't have been? This was the last day of hearings in the case and it was evident that the judge was pushing to get through with the proceedings as quickly as possible.

Mr. Benson told Margie, "This is extremely unusual procedure. I promise."

"I will retire to my chamber to ponder the fate of these four children. Court is now in recess and will reconvene in one hour."

Benson leaned over and whispered to Margie, "Judge is acting weird. I think I smell a rat somewhere."

"Do you mean one other than the rat I spent eleven years of my life with?" He shrugged as he took a deep breath.

An hour later, as Margie sat with Mr. Benson at the desk in front of the court room, Jose sat with his attorney, Ed Smerling. Rose, Tony, Anna and Karen sat with Emma in the court room, the Judge's gavel pounding the podium, BANG, BANG, BANG! "After giving the situation much careful consideration and deliberation, the only conclusion I can arrive at is that the interest of these four children will be best served if custody is awarded to their father."

"Uh!" Gasps and grumblings were heard all over the court room.

The judge banged the gavel again. "Order! I will award custody, but only on a temporary basis. Mr. Rivera, you are not to leave the county or the state with the children unless you have obtained permission from the court. Is that understood?"

Jose clenched his teeth and stared daggers through the judge, "Yes, your Honor! Understood."

"This court is dismissed." The judge pounded his gavel again.

In complete and utter shock, Margie sobbed brokenly and leaned her head on her attorney's arm, "Most of those things they said about me were lies. Maybe not everything, but most were. I know that that Latin Dudley Do Right paid every last one of those witnesses to lie about me. What about all the rotten things he did when he was overseas?" At that point, she could not control her emotions at all, nor did she want to.

While Margie was still reeling from the blow she had been dealt by the fair and unbiased judicial system, she had yet another blow dealt to her. Two courtroom attendants came out of nowhere and tried to wrestle away her four young children from Emma who, along with Clarence had been sitting faithfully behind Margie during the courtroom proceedings. Emma was indignant with the attendants, "What in tarnation do you think you're doing? Get your hands off of my grandkids, you oversized barnyard bullies." She tried to intervene and stop the men from taking the children away by pulling the children in one direction while the attendants tugged in the opposite direction.

Amidst all the confusion, the two youngest, Karen and Anna, commenced crying and whining. Tears streamed down Karen's face as she chewed on her little fist. Anna put on the brave face of an older sister and tried to comfort her, "It's okay, Sissy. Everyting's alwight."

While Rose was the oldest daughter, she was still totally freaked out. She loved her mother more than anything on earth, and she realized that the court room goons were trying to take her away from her mom.

She rebelled by first biting the hand of the attendant who had grabbed her arm, then she made a mad dash for her mom, while her older brother Tony looked on the entire scene in absolute silence.

Margie, heartbroken, knelt, opening her arms wide and Rose ran into her embrace. Rose threw her arms around her mother's neck, wailing, "I love you, Mommy. I love you. Please don't let them take us! Please!" The poor girl was on the verge of hysteria by now.

Margie could barely speak without choking on her words, "I am so sorry, sweetheart." She was shaking so badly that she had to take a deep breath before she could go on. "I love you very much too. It will only be for a little while, sweetheart. I promise, only for a little while." As Margie heard herself speak the words to her daughter, she could only hope that her words were true—that it would be only for a little while.

Anna and Karen gathered around their mother, sobbing and crying in unison, "I love you Mommy. I don't want to go." Margie thought her heart would break in two. She gathered her two youngest children in her arms and held them close while fighting back the tears.

Tony had stood by and watched in silence, helpless to stop the pain he could so easily see his younger sisters and his mother were going through. He was last to approach his mother. He put on his bravest face for her. "It's okay Mom. I'll…I'll…I'll watch out for the girls."

The Ancient Paths

He gave her a hug, and with that, the four children were whisked away from their mother's embrace.

CHAPTER 3

Rose wore an apron tied around her small body and she was standing in the kitchen chair washing dishes. Tony was busy ironing clothes while the two younger sisters played pat-a-cake. The front door opened quietly, so the children did not really notice when their father arrived home at their duplex. Jose stepped into the kitchen, all smiles. "I have someone I would like for you guys to meet," he announced. Out from behind Jose stepped Edwina, who was blond, very attractive and shapely. She smiled warmly at the children, as they stared blankly back at her. She couldn't help but notice that the children looked tired, confused and even a little pitiful.

Then, to add to the children's surprise of meeting their father's new love interest, out from behind Edwina came one, two, three girls, and then a boy! The oldest of Edwina's girls was Kelly, then there was Sharon, next was Alana, and last but not least was Gerald, her only son. Just like Jose, Edwina had one son and three daughters; only, her daughters were a little bit older than Jose's children. Edwina's children ranged in age from fifteen years old to about age seven.

Tony, Rose, Anna and Karen still had not spoken. The eight children just stood, staring at one another, none of them knowing exactly what

28

to say. Then Jose made his announcement. "Guess what, you guys. Edwina and her children are moving in with us. Isn't that great?"

Rose and Tony continued to stare blankly at their father. They were not able to comprehend where 10 people were going to sleep in a 2-bedroom duplex. "Daddy, where will everyone sleep?" Rose asked.

"Shut up, stupid! That's none of your business. Just do what you're told, Rose," Jose hissed at her. "We won't be staying at this place long. We have a better place to move to."

So, for the next several months, Jose and Edwina shared a bed in Jose's room, while the eight children shared two queen sized beds, a rollaway bed, and a cot. Rose often found herself wondering when they were going to move to that "better place." Or, did such a place even exist?

***

After dinner, Jose pulled aside Tony and Kelly, the two oldest of each family. He reached into his pocket and withdrew his wallet, from which he extracted several dollar bills. "Why don't you two take everyone to the Dairy Dip, and we'll meet you guys there in a little while." Tony and Kelly eagerly accepted the money and quickly set out to round up the rest of the children in order that they might begin the walk to the Dairy Dip. It was rare for them to have treats of any kind during those days, much less ice cream!

The Ancient Paths

As the eight children made their way through the neighborhood streets, evening began to cast its shadow. Tony carried Karen on his hip, and to the stranger passing by in a car, this little group of vagabonds silhouetted under the glow of the streetlights, appeared to be a group of the young and homeless. "I wonder what's really going on," Kelly pondered out loud to Tony.

"What do you mean?"

"You know what I'm talking about. Your dad is being a little too nice, don't you think? He NEVER gives us money."

"Yeah, I know. He's never nice either, is he? Oops! Never mind. I didn't say that!" Kelly laughed at Tony's slip of the tongue. "Don't worry, Tony. I won't say anything. I wouldn't say anything, because you're right."

At the Dairy Dip, everyone had settled on top of the picnic table outside and were chowing down on their favorite ice cream treat when Jose and Edwina arrived in the station wagon. To the amazement of the children, there were large suitcases tied to the top of the vehicle with rope. Jose jumped out of the car, "Hurry, hurry, everyone. Jump in." No one dared argue with him.

With looks of bewilderment on their faces, they all simply quietly obeyed. Everyone that is, except Rose. "Daddy, where are we going?"

"It's a surprise. Yep. That's it. We have a big surprise for you guys. So, now get in the car and stop your yapping!" Rose skeptically complied. She could tell that he had no patience for this line of questioning at the moment.

After driving all night and what seemed like an eternity, the caravan of ten arrived in a large, sprawling, dirty city, the likes of which the children had never seen before. It was early in the day, just after dawn, and the eight children were irritable after the long, cramped drive from Nashville, Tennessee.

"Okay, guys, here we are. Let's get out."

The kids all had turned down mouths. Everyone was tired and achy after the cramped drive, and they did not know where "here" was supposed to be. So, Rose asked the obvious question, "Where is here, Daddy?"

"Rose, you are always asking questions when you should keep your trap shut! But, for your information, we are here, and here is Binghamton, New York."

"Ah!" All of the children gasped at once, even Karen and Anna, who were not even old enough to know what a New York was.

The Ancient Paths

The children slowly and sleepily made their way out of the car, only to have the reality hit them like a ton of bricks that in front of them loomed a large tenement slum building which ran the length of a city block. There were children playing hopscotch and jump rope out on the sidewalk; but, make no mistake about it, this was a dump, with a capital D. Karen and Anna began to whine. They were scared and had no idea what had just happened to them. Neither did Rose and Tony for that matter. To be exact, in legal terms, what had actually happened was that Jose had just *kidnapped* his children by taking them out of state while under court orders not to even take the children out of the county without obtaining permission from the court first. Oh, the lengths a parent will go to for parental love. Was it parental love or was it the desire to exact revenge on an ex-spouse?

Karen whimpered again. "I want Mommy."

Jose snapped, "Shut your sister's trap, Rose!" Edwina and her children looked uncomfortably at one another. What had Edwina gotten them all into?

"Jose, don't you think you're being a little hard on the children?"

The light of reason illuminated and softened Jose's eyes. "I don't know, perhaps. I'm just tired. Let's go inside and see our new home."

The caravan of ten climbed the long flight of stairs to the entrance of the apartment building, while clusters of children continued to play hopscotch and jump rope in this inner-city neighborhood.

The living arrangements at their new home were not any better than the small duplex which they had left behind. Here there was only one bedroom, and that belonged to Jose and Edwina. The children would all sleep in beds and on mattresses in the large living room.

The children were quickly enrolled in the local schools. One day while all of the children were in class, there was an announcement over the school intercom. "I am sorry to Announce today that our President, John F. Kennedy, has been assassinated. He was fatally wounded by a gunman today in Dallas, Texas."

At hearing the news, Rose's teacher wept openly in front of the class. Rose quickly raised her hand to ask a question. "What does that mean, Miss Franish?"

"Rose, I'm afraid it means our President has been killed."

As the realization of what their teacher was saying began to dawn on them, that the life of the leader of their country had suddenly been taken, the girls in the class felt fearful and small, so they cried. Suddenly, everyone was crying, and school was dismissed early in order for everyone to go home and be with their families.

The Ancient Paths

That evening at home, Edwina could not help but be a little sad. "Jose, what's going on? Everything is spinning out of control. We're here in New York, in this crowded apartment with eight kids, you're working as a janitor, and our President has just been shot. What in the world does all this mean?"

"So, you're not happy, then? You think my job is a dead end job, and that I can't provide a decent living for all of us? Is that it?"

"No, that isn't it at all, Jose. I mean, we're about to go into the holiday season, and this thing with our President being assassinated today has really made me wonder what we're all doing here so far away from the rest of our family members."

"I don't have any family," he said, and they both lapsed into silence.

As Christmas Day drew nearer, the Christmas tree was placed in the living room, and the older children made decorations by stringing cranberries and popcorn before adding the final touch of garland, and the younger children were in awe of how beautiful the tree looked with such simple decorations. Edwina rocked serenely in her rocking chair while sewing a rip in one of Jose's pairs of pants. She silently watched him out of the corner of her eye as he repeatedly stole glances at her daughters over the book he was reading. It was snowing outside, and the snow helped set the mood as everyone was trying to get into the Christmas spirit. But, then, the peace was to be only temporary.

The Ancient Paths

Anna and Karen were seated on the couch, and together they watched the older children making strands of popcorn and cranberries. Kelly leaned over and whispered to Tony, "When is your dad going to marry my mom?"

Tony shrugged, "Maybe never, if she's real lucky."

Kelly whispered, "That would suit me just fine."

Amidst all the small talk and activity in the room, no one except Jose noticed when Anna slowly and silently slid down from the couch; and as she did, Jose's eyes fell on the round wet spot which had been left on the couch. Anna tried her best to leave the room unnoticed, but Jose was not having it.

In the blink of an eye, Jose was up and on his feet. His voice stopped her dead in her little tracks. "What is that, Anna?" He was pointing at the wet ring she had left behind. She had only recently graduated from wearing diapers. She had not been completely potty trained, but everyone had agreed that she was ready for big girl underwear. In one fell swoop, Jose picked the child up, turned her upside down and began rubbing her nose in the wet spot, despite her cries of protest.

Edwina screamed at him over the screams of Anna. "Stop it, Jose. Put her down!" He glared at Edwina as everyone in the room sat watching in disbelief. He snarled at Edwina, "This is none of your business! She's my child, not yours! Stay out of this!"

Jose ran from the room with poor Anna still in his arms, while she continued screaming and crying; only, now she was turned right side up. As Jose entered the bathroom with Anna still in his arm, he turned her upside down yet again; only this time, he tried to shove her head into the toilet bowl. The child struggled to try and keep her head from going in as she grabbed the edge of the commode in order to resist. Struggle as she may, Jose's physical strength was too much for Anna. She lost her grip, and her head hit the toilet water. The splash could be heard in the next room. As soon as she was brought up out of the water by her heels and was able to gasp for air, her father ducked her head into the toilet water a second time. But, getting her little head soaked in toilet bowl water was not good enough for Jose. No, not quite good enough. With one hand, he grabbed the toilet handle and flushed the commode while he held Anna with his other hand, with her head still in the toilet, completely terrorizing the child, as she wept and repeatedly begged, "No, Daddy! Please, Daddy!" She thought she was about to be flushed down the toilet.

Jose had not noticed that Edwina had entered the restroom as well. She was suddenly on him, pulling him back, away from the toilet, as Anna's head came up out of the wet bowl. Edwina was screaming, "I said stop it! For God's sake, Jose, stop. She's your daughter. What kind of animal are you, anyway?" As suddenly as he had started, Jose stopped his brutal attack on the girl and sat her down on the floor as he collapsed into a little heap on the floor and sobbed uncontrollably.

In the living room, the other children sat stone faced, frozen like statues, staring questioningly at one another. Rose whispered, "I want to go home. I miss my mother."

The following day was Saturday. Gone was the Christmas spirit which everyone had felt for a brief moment the evening before. When Rose woke up that morning, she sat up in the bed, looked around, saw that the other seven children were still asleep, and decided to get up anyway. Quietly she made her way to her clothes drawer, slipped on her play clothes, put on her boots, picked up her coat, tiptoed down the hallway, peeked into her father's room long enough to see that he and Edwina were still asleep, then she opened the front door quietly and slipped out to play.

CHAPTER 4

As always happens, and has always happened since the beginning of time, winter turned to spring; and what a relief it was for the children to be able to go outside without having to put on two layers of clothing. The spring in New York was still much cooler than what they had known in Tennessee, but it was a welcome break after such a long, grueling winter.

Rose played hopscotch by herself as two young boys, Howie and Willie watched her from the sidelines. Tony, Kelly and the rest of the gang were hanging out on the long flight of steps in the front of the tenement building. Howie and Willie were mesmerized by Rose, but she was totally oblivious to them.

Howie yelled at Willie, "She's my girlfriend!"

"She is not! She's mine!" Willie yelled back.

"Is not." Howie did not give up easily. And just like that, Willie clobbered Howie, and an all-out fist fight ensued between the two boys.

As the flurry of activity buzzed around Rose, she spied an older woman, Miz Minnie, atop the flight of steps of the adjoining building. Miz Minnie wore a long green, floral print dress which came two thirds of the way to her ankles, and black shoes which were laced up with old fashioned, thick black heels. She had light olive skin, gray hair, a face full of wrinkles and the kindest brown eyes Rose had ever seen. The little old lady waved to Rose. "Rose, I need you for a little while. Can you please help me?" Without saying a word, Rose headed toward Miz Minnie when Sharon and Kelly noticed where she was headed and tried to intervene. They jumped up from their seat on the steps and ran to Rose before she had time to step foot on the bottom of the staircase which lead all the way up to Miz Minnie.

Kelly spoke with authority, "Don't go up there, Rose."

But Rose was not easily deterred, "Why not?"

"Because…because she's the Candy Witch, that's why." Kelly interjected.

Rose looked thoughtfully from one of the girls to the other, but somehow, she was fast enough that she managed to slip between the sisters and was on the stairs headed toward Miz Minnie before they could stop her. She paused and turned to look at them briefly. "Well, she's my friend and she's very nice to me so I'm gonna help her." With that, Rose hurried to attend to Miz Minnie.

39

The Ancient Paths

***

Inside Miz Minnie's apartment, the decorations were exactly like what one would expect to see in the home of an older woman living alone. Dusty, yellowed lace curtains covered her windows. Corner shelves, windowsills, trays placed atop radiators, every conceivable surface was covered with hundreds of figurines, bric-a-brac and just plain old junk. The tic-tock of her antique grandfather clock filled the silence of the room, as the pendulum swung back and forth…back and forth. A longhaired gray cat slept next to Miz Minnie's feet as she softly rocked to and fro, while the scent of burning sticks of incense wafted through the still apartment air.

Rose sat cozily on the couch and enjoyed a stick of hard peppermint candy as Miz Minnie rocked steadily back and forth while she knitted. "Rose, you are different from them. They are naughty children and you are such a good girl."

"Who's naughty, Miz Minnie?"

Perhaps it was her senility, or perhaps because she really didn't know herself who she was talking about, but Miz Minnie never answered her, she just kept on talking. "You should stay away from them. I will pray for you, my little Rose, and perhaps you should pray for the others. Come over here to Miz Minnie, Rose." Rose crawled down from the couch and stopped directly in front of Miz Minnie. The old lady lovingly touched Rose's hair and cupped her chin in her hand. "One day you will see, Rose. You are different. How is your father?"

Rose dropped her head noticeably and lowered her voice. "He's just fine, Miz Minnie." The old lady could see by Rose's body language that all was not well. For the first time, Miz Minnie noticed the bruised place on Rose's neck.

"Miz Minnie, the children aren't naughty. It's my daddy who's naughty." Rose could no longer hold back the tears, and they began to flow freely down her little cheeks.

"I know he is dear. But, when you get older, you will see that there are lots of naughty people. You need to try to stay a good girl, and don't become one of those bad people."

Rose became visibly upset. "I won't, Miz Minnie. I promise. I don't want to be like my daddy. I don't want to be bad."

Miz Minnie turned to her right and removed something from a small jewelry box. "Miz Minnie wants to give you something, Rose." The old lady reached for Rose's hand and dropped whatever it was she had removed from the jewelry box into Rose's hand. Rose was so excited that she quickly wrapped her little hand around the gift. When Rose realized that Miz Minnie was waiting for her to look at the gift, she slowly opened up her fingers to reveal an antique locket which showed

41

a picture of Jesus' face. Miz Minnie, in her ancient mannerism, reached forward, cupped Rose's face in her hand again, and recited Numbers 6:24-26 from the King James Bible, "The Lord bless you and keep you. The Lord make his face shine upon you and be gracious to you. The Lord lift up his countenance upon you and give you peace. I will keep you in my prayers, young Rose."

CHAPTER 5

Jose stepped out of the stairwell and slowly made his way down the hallway to the front door of the apartment, reached into his pocket for the key and unlocked the door. Except for the children's books which lay scattered on the couch from the evening before, the living room was void of all signs of life, and he couldn't help but notice how quiet the apartment was. "Good," he thought, "I can rest for a while before everyone gets home." He relaxed on the couch for a moment, removed his shoes, then tiredly pulled himself off the couch and left the room.

Kelly who had already arrived home from school, showered, and was clad in only a towel and rubbing lotion on her face when the door unexpectedly jarred open. Her response was fear, and her first impulse was to scream, and she did.

Jose stopped for a second, his mouth gaped open, somewhat stunned and scrutinized her carefully. "Why...why didn't you lock the door?"

Kelly was both embarrassed and frightened. "I thought I was by myself. What are you doing here anyway?"

"I, uh...got off work early. Where is everybody?" Their attention

43

turned toward the door when Edwina opened the door further and stepped in the room. Her expression, which was one of shock, said it all. Jose quickly tried to explain, "Edwina, it's not what you think. Nothing happened. I swear, nothing." She did not say one word, but hurried from the room feeling hurt, disgust and disappointment.

The next day Edwina and Jose stood facing each other as her children boarded the bus whose sign read NASHVILLE. "Edwina, please don't go. Nothing ever happened. Please stay and we'll get married. I promise."

"I'm sorry, Jose. I'm afraid it's a little too late for that. I can't live in your world any longer. But, I will keep my promise, and not tell anyone where you and your children are after I arrive back in Nashville. But, Jose, so help me God, if I ever hear of you harming a hair on those kids' heads again, I will talk so fast that you will be locked up for good." She kissed Jose on the cheek and boarded the bus, as a lone, silent tear made its way down Jose's face.

"She may be the only woman I ever truly loved," he thought to himself as he waved goodbye.

The following day as Jose swept the floors of the bowling alley where he worked, and as he thought of Edwina, he was approached by a man in a business suit who was accompanied by a second man also in a suit who was smoking a cigar.

"Jose, didn't you say that you have your engineering degree?" "Why, yes, I did, Harvey."

"Well then, why are you working in this godforsaken place, man? I hate to lose a good employee, Jose, and you have been a good one, but it's obvious to me this place is not for you. You need to be using that education of yours. This is my friend, Roger Zimmerman, and he has an opening at the company he manages."

Jose's mouth was still gaping wide open, as this act of kindness had caught him totally off guard. Mr. Zimmerman shook Jose's hand with a firm, confident grip while he handed Jose a business card with his other hand. Mr. Zimmerman found out that it was difficult talking, shaking hands, and smoking a cigar all at the same time. "Harvey has told me a lot of good things about you, Mr. Rivera. If you can bring me your resume tomorrow, I may have a proposition for you."

"Why, yes, of course. How can I thank you, Harvey? Mr. Zimmerman, how does eleven o'clock tomorrow sound?"

"I will see you then, Jose." They shook hands again, and just like that, Roger Zimmerman and Harvey went their own way.

Everything had happened so quickly that he wasn't quite sure exactly what all had in fact just transpired. All Jose did know was that he had sacrificed his career as a staff sergeant in the military to come to the rescue of his children, and now he had laid a golden egg, and nothing was going to get in his way. You see, in his mind at least, Jose was the only one who cared about his four poor, misfortunate children. After all, he had rescued them from that young country bumpkin wife of his and her hillbilly relatives. He was their dad, so he must know what was best for his children. Right?

CHAPTER 6

Jose stepped outside of the court house. He had done it. He had signed the papers, now all he had to do was wait. He had landed the job as electrical engineer; it was a done deal. Now all he had to do was deal with this last piece of business.

The following afternoon, there was a knock on the door of the apartment. "Somebody get that, please," Jose yelled from the back room. Tony heaved a sigh and obediently opened the door. In front of him stood a woman in professional attire whom he had never seen before. She wore her hair pulled back in a tight bun, had on a long skirt which came halfway between her knees and her ankles, wore black thick heeled shoes, and carried a briefcase. Her very presence was imposing. Tony wasn't sure what to say, so he didn't say anything.

"Can I come in, please?" She did not wait for an answer, but barged past the door and into the apartment. Jose emerged from the back room. "Mr. Rivera?"

"Yes."

"Hi. I'm Mrs. Kraus from the Department of Children's Services." Tony and Rose looked at one another bewildered. What was going on?

"Have you had a chance to discuss this with your children yet?"

"No, I'm afraid I haven't."

In unison Tony and Rose queried, "Tell us what, Daddy?"

Jose knelt on one knee and looked at his two oldest children with a glimmer of sorrow. "Guys, I don't know how else to tell you this, but because I need to work a lot now to save some money to buy a home for us, and I have no one to take care of you, I must let you all go to a foster home for a while."

Rose was astonished. "Uh! Not again. We did that before yours and Mommy's divorce."

The social worker interrupted. "Mr. Rivera, perhaps it would help if they knew that they will be together in their new home. We found an elderly couple who has another foster child already living with them. This should be the perfect situation for everyone."

The children were reeling from the blur that had become their life! First their parents divorced, then their father moved in his new girlfriend and her four children; then they were uprooted from their mother and their familiar surroundings in Tennessee and taken to New York where they discovered that their father was less then gentle when it came to doling out punishment. As if that was not enough, Edwina, the new mother image they had become accustomed to, and her children who had become like family, had up and left them with their father who was never happy a day in his life and returned to Tennessee, where Tony and Rose knew their mother was, and now they were going to their second foster home. How unfair could life get for four young and innocent lives anyway? A perfect situation? What in the heck was that?

"The children will be taken to their new home today."

It was Saturday, and the children had looked forward to playing outside with their friends. "I don't want to go. I just want to play with Howie and Willie, Daddy."

"Rose, stop it. Do not disrespect me. You must go, all of you. This is no place for someone to raise their children. You must get out while you can. I will pack some of your clothes to take with you today, and I will bring the rest to you later, including your new toys you got for Christmas."

The two youngest girls started crying, as they too had the realization that they would be taken away yet again. While the situation with their father was less than ideal, at this time in their life, being with their father was the only 'home' they all knew. Tony tried to comfort his little sisters. "It's okay, girls. We'll all be together, so I can look out for you and Rose. Okay?" The little girls nodded their heads in unison as they held hands and tried to put on a brave face for their brother.

CHAPTER 7

It was late afternoon, the wind was picking up momentum, and the snow drifts were growing more intense. It was Mrs. Kraus, not Jose, who delivered the four children to the home of Mr. and Mrs. Barrett that cold, gray winter day in the late afternoon. When Mrs. Kraus knocked on the door, a short, heavyset, be-speckled woman with curly salt and peppered hair was who opened the door to greet them. It was hard for the children to determine what they felt about this woman at first sight. In a way, she looked like she could have been anybody's grandmother. However, to be more exact, she was actually a very homely woman who was so plain that it was difficult to find anything soft or feminine in her features. Her glasses were thick and black, and she seemed to wear a scowl behind what was obviously a forced smile. The children were somewhat startled by her appearance, as they had never actually seen a woman who was quite as plain as her. Even Mrs. Kraus, for all of her look of harshness behind the tightly pulled back bun and professional looking spectacles, was a softer and more feminine woman than this lady.

Mrs. Kraus extended her hand to the woman; however, the woman did not shake Mrs. Kraus's gloved hand, instead she quickly brushed off Mrs. Kraus's attempt to be cordial. She seemed to have no time for such niceties.

"Mrs. Barrett, here are your new wards. These are Tony, Rose, Anna and Karen. I have told them that they will have a foster brother while staying here. What was his name again?"

"His name is Kevin. But, won't you come in, *please*?" Mrs. Barrett gritted her teeth when she spoke, as it was an effort for her to be pleasant to *anyone,* even another adult. It was only too obvious that it was just an afterthought for her to tack on the word 'please' at the end of her sentence. So, with that, the group of five stepped inside the warm and cozy home. Odd, the house itself seemed to exude more warmth than its owner! The siblings were all a bit dazed and confused from being shuffled from one circumstance to the other so often in their young lives. They always tried to just listen to what was being said and do what they were told.

Mrs. Kraus held some of the small luggage the children had brought with them, while Tony and Rose carried the rest. But, once she had set down the pieces she carried, Mrs. Kraus wasted no time in making her exit. "Children, your father will be able to visit you from time to time. I will also be checking in with you on occasion to see how you are doing. But, I must leave now. And, by the way, Happy New Year." It was New Year's Eve. So, just like that Mrs. Kraus left their lives as quickly as she had entered. The children would soon learn that Mrs. Kraus would never stop by for those promised visits, nor would their father be coming for visits.

As the children surveyed their new surroundings, everything *appeared* to be warm and cozy and normal. However, Rose's youthful and not yet developed insight still told her this was not a normal home. The kitchen seemed to be the main room where people would enter the home from the road, as opposed to the living room being the main entryway. Pots and pans lined one of the walls in the kitchen, the smell of coffee permeated the air, and floral laced curtains decorated the window which was over the kitchen sink. Past the kitchen was the dining room, which was small, but had a bit of a formal air to it; then there was the living room where the man of the house, Mr. Barrett, sat watching the television. He was long and thin. His hair was short and was also salt and peppered like his wife's. His face was long and thin, just like his body, and he too seemed to have trouble smiling. He managed to mutter a brief, "Hello. Welcome." He looked like a kind and quiet elderly gentleman, but his attention was quickly diverted back to sports. It was hard not to notice the baby grand piano in the corner of the living room. Rose had always wanted to learn the piano.

Mrs. Barrett turned her head in the other direction and yelled, "Kevin! Get down here! It's time to meet your new foster brother and sisters!" She looked at the four children and said, "You'll love Kevin. He's a very um…*special* boy." What did "special" mean? They all wondered. Footsteps could be heard bounding down the steps from the second level of the house, and then there was Kevin. Kevin was a tall, skinny, homely kid who wore black horn rimmed glasses, had buck teeth, and had an undeniable twitch." He was sort of goofy looking, actually. So this was what "special" meant?

"Hey, guys. Boy, am I glad to have some other kids here to talk to. Come on and I'll show you where your rooms are." He appeared to be a very upbeat kid for someone who lived in a foster home.

"Kevin," Mrs. Barrett interrupted, "Karen will be sleeping in the little room downstairs. She's so small that she needs to be downstairs where we can keep an eye on her."

"Uh, okay."

In the absence of Mrs. Kraus, Tony and Rose carried the bags of the smaller girls since they were simply too small to carry their own. Kevin didn't bother to ask if he could help. They dropped off Karen's belongings in the small bedroom downstairs, which was at the foot of the staircase leading upstairs to the other rooms.

"Well, Karen, you're a big girl that gets to have your own room," Rose chirped, trying to make her little sister feel better about being in a room by herself. She knew that Karen would want to be with her and Anna, but she could see that it was not going to happen.

Next, the group of five children made their way up the staircase which ended in a big open area room that had two other rooms extending from it. Kevin pointed at the rooms. "Tony, this will be mine and your room. This other room is Anna and Rose's. That's pretty much it."

Rose thought aloud, "But, there is enough room for Karen to sleep up here with us. So, why can't she?"

Kevin shrugged his shoulders. "I don't know. I just do whatever Mrs. Barrett says. She's the boss around here. Her husband just sits back and tries to be quiet." The children would quickly learn just how quiet Mr. Barrett could be.

"Hey, you guys want to go outside and play in the snow?" Kevin asked. He wanted to be entertaining and hospitable, it seemed. Even though the four children were still in shock from being moved yet again, they were eager to burn off some energy and frustration. "I'll have to ask Mrs. Barrett if it's okay first," Kevin explained. Before anyone could blink an eye, Kevin ran downstairs and was back in the next blink of an eye. "She said okay, but we have to come back inside in an hour and get ready for dinner."

Anna and Karen couldn't help but show their excitement and clapped their little hands. "Yay!"

So, one by one, the group of five made their way down the stairs, out the back door of the house, which was actually the living room door, and into the big back yard which was covered in snow three feet deep! The Barrett's had never shoveled their back yard this season. What a heyday the kids had, smashing each other in the face with snowballs, and poor Karen and Anna were so small and light that they practically glided over the snow. During the course of exploring the far corners of the back yard, Rose's boot came off in the snow, and she couldn't find it! The snow was so deep that she wasn't able to see that boot again no matter how hard she looked. "Oh boy, I know I'm in trouble," she said.

When the children went back in the house, Mrs. Barrett did not try to hide the fact that she was upset about Rose having lost her boot. "What do you mean, taking off your shoes outside in weather like this? Don't you know how expensive boots are, young lady?"

Rose stood at attention with her eyes bulging in her head and tried not to breathe. "Yes ma'am. I'm sorry. I didn't take my boot off. It just got stuck in the snow."

"Well, get yourself upstairs, get dried off and get ready for supper. The rest of you get ready for dinner too." With that, everyone scrambled to exit from her presence as quickly as they possibly could. Mr. Barrett sat quietly reading the paper, and never looked up.

Tony, Rose, Anna and Karen were ravenous! They had not eaten a home cooked meal since Edwina had left town with her children, and they couldn't wait for dinner. Once everyone had arrived at the dinner table, Mrs. Barrett directed everyone to the seat they were to sit in. For dinner, they were having green peas, carrots, Salisbury steak and rolls. This suited everyone fine, except for Anna, who had never adapted her palette to include a liking for green peas. When everyone had completed dinner and left the table, Anna asked if she could be excused too.

"No ma'am. You have to eat every last bite of food on your plate before you can get up," Mrs. Barrett instructed. Anna wanted to, but the taste of the peas made her nauseous. When Mrs. Barrett left the room to start taking dinner plates to the kitchen, Anna held her hand down for the Chihuahua, Barky, to nibble on the peas she held in her hand. Every time Mrs. Barrett left, Barky would get another handful of peas. Slowly but surely, by bedtime, Anna had successfully completed the task of getting rid of all her peas, and she was finally able to get up and run to the bathroom, since she had held her kidneys now for over two hours.

New Year's Day came and went. Once again, winter turned to spring, and the world took on a different appearance. The first full day of warm weather, after the older children arrived home from school, they all ran outside yelling and squealing, playing tag and swinging on the old tire swing out back. It was obvious that they were ready for the change in the weather. Mrs. Barrett observed the kids from a distance, inside the living room. "Thank goodness for warm days. I could not stand one more day with those brats cooped up in here," she grumbled.

Mr. Barrett sat reading his paper while she talked. "Um hum," was all she could get out of him. She was fuming. No one ever paid her any attention. What did everyone think she was? Mother Goose or something? Suddenly, as she watched the children laughing, playing, skipping and holding hands, Mrs. Barrett decided that the children didn't need to be outside after all. They were having way too much fun to suit her. She went outside and called the kids to come inside and wash up.

"But, we are having fun. Can we please stay outside and play?" Karen begged as she simultaneously clapped her hands and jumped up and down like a little Mexican jumping bean. Mrs. Barrett looked down at the small child and noted her beautiful smile and her look of joy and excitement; then without any hint of a conscience whatsoever, her hand slowly raised, then came down suddenly as she backhanded the child and sent her reeling. Karen's body spun around twice before she stumbled and fell to the ground. It happened so quickly that the child did not have time to even catch her breath. Tony, Rose and Anna rushed to her side. The child was obviously shaken and heartbroken.

"What did you have to do that for, you old hag? She didn't do nothing to you. She's just a little girl!" Tony roared. He was so angry that she could almost see the bolts of lightning emanating from the boy's dark brown glaring eyes. Kevin chose to stand back and observe. He did not want to be in the middle of this confrontation. After all, in spite of his sweet personality, the boy happened to have a yellow streak that ran the length of the state of California, and he had demons of his own.

Mrs. Barrett pointed her finger in Tony's face, "You, young man, watch your mouth. Don't even think about testing me. And, as your punishment for sassing me, you can feed Mr. Butts tonight." Tony's jaw dropped in disbelief. Mr. Butts was a wild, untamed **BABOON!** Mrs. Barrett kept him in a huge cage inside the garage. She called him "her baby!" The animal was strong enough to rip someone apart.

When Rose heard this, she came and stood between Tony and Mrs. Barrett. "Tony, don't. Let me talk to her." Then Rose turned to Mrs. Barrett and screamed at her, "You old witch! You leave my baby sister and my brother alone! I hate you!" Well, that really made things better. As much as she wanted to hit Rose, Mrs. Barrett knew that she was psychologically outnumbered at the moment, as the bond between the four siblings was stronger than any bond she had ever seen in a family, even stronger than the bond between her and her own son.

Mrs. Barrett retreated to the house while Tony, Rose and Anna helped their little sister up off the ground, put their arms around her and tried to comfort her. In the final analysis, it seemed that in this world of cruel and uncontrollable events, each other was all they really had.

All the while, Mr. Barrett had been quietly observing all of the commotion through the bay window in the living room. Mrs. Barrett stormed into the living room and made her way to the bench of the old church piano and sat down. At first, she slowly moved her fingers across the keys and the sounds of peaceful classic church hymns filled the air. But soon, the tone changed from serene to insane as her fingers moved faster and harder over the keys, and the music mutated into echoes of something resembling horror film music. Still, Mr. Barrett did not speak. He only watched and listened.

Mrs. Barrett gave Tony instructions that evening before sending him into the garage to feed Mr. Butts. "There is a bag of food in the corner. Just use the tin cup on the inside of the bag to get one large scoop, then slowly unlock the small window of the cage and pour the food into the bowl, then close the window and lock it back."

When he entered the garage, Tony scooped up a serving of the animal feed in the metal cup. He had to work his way around to the backside of the cage, as that was where the small window was. The window was nothing more than a small section of the wire cage which opened up to the food bowl. Tony ever so slightly opened the door and reached his hand through to feed Mr. Butts. Mr. Butts had managed to reach his arms through the wires of the cage, and as Tony closed the small opening in the cage, the baboon grabbed Tony's arm and began screaming and pulling. The baboon had the strength of two men. Tony struggled to pull away from Mr. Butts grip, as Mr. Butts was opening and closing his mouth repeatedly trying to bite him through the wire cage. "You stupid ape!" Tony yelled. Finally, Tony wrestled free, but not before his nerves had been seriously rattled and his shirt sleeve torn to shreds. Mrs. Barrett stood outside the garage door observing the entire incident, and grinned. She believed she had made her point.

And, so life went in their new home. Mrs. Barrett was all about abuse and nastiness, Mr. Butts was an ape, Kevin was sweet but possibly somewhat mentally challenged and Mr. Barrett was always silent. Even though all of the children believed that Mr. Barrett was a good man, as he was not like his wife, they had learned that Mr. Barrett could never be counted on to speak up and defend them against his wife, so they ceased to even consider him as a possible rescuer. Their father had yet to show up and bring them the rest of their clothes and toys; so, how could they tell him? And besides, would he even care? And Mrs. Kraus? Well, she was just a name and face of the past.

Up to this point, on the surface at least, Kevin seemed to have bonded well with the four siblings. He was *okay* for a foster brother. Only, there still was something not quite right about the boy. He was always wrinkling up his face and scrooching up his nose, pushing back his glasses from where they always slid to the bottom of his nose; and he had that eternal nervous twitch. He was also Mrs. Barrett's favorite. He was sweet and all, but he always managed to get on someone's nerves. None of the kids could quite put their finger on it, but it soon became obvious that Kevin was not exactly wired like the rest of the children. Perhaps part of the reason for that may have been because Kevin was *not* their sibling, or in other words, he was not from the same mold; therefore, he was not wired like the rest of the children.

Rose had begun to blossom into a very young lady. She was just beginning to be little more than a child, but she was the first of the girls to show any sign of maturing, since she was the oldest. It happened on more than one occasion that she noticed Kevin openly gawking at her, and this made her a little uncomfortable. Why did he stare at her like that? She wondered.

It was spring time, as you know. Rose found some rose petals which had fallen to the ground. The smell of the petals was so wonderful that she did not want to lose them. She found a tiny white box, placed the red petals in the box and sat them in her window sill. Every day she would check the small box of petals and inhale the fragrance. This, she thought, was the greatest discovery since the rose itself.

One day while Anna and Karen were gone to the store with Mrs. Barrett, and Tony was at a friend's house, as Rose sat by the window pondering the rose petals, she could not ignore the feeling that maybe she was not alone. When she looked up, what she saw was shocking, to say the least. There in the middle of the upstairs, clad in absolutely nothing was Kevin. "Oh my gosh!" she screamed. "Get your clothes on, Kevin. What's wrong with you? Ooh!" She quickly ran out of her bedroom, past Kevin and downstairs. As always, Mr. Barrett sat watching television with his newspaper in his lap. Rose ran outside and swung on the tire swing in order to get away from Kevin, and to avoid saying anything to Mr. Barrett. And later, she dared not breathe a word of the incident to Mrs. Barrett, as she did not want to get Kevin in deep water with her. So, she told Tony instead.

"He did what?" Tony was incredulous. "I will beat his butt," Tony said very matter of factly.

"No, Tony. Don't do that. Mrs. Barrett will probably only get mad at you, and find some crazy way to punish you, or both us for that matter. I don't even really want to get Kevin in trouble. I just want him to stop."

So in lieu of kicking his butt, Tony decided he would speak to Kevin about his behavior toward his sister. "Kevin, listen, man. You're my friend, and you're a friend to all my sisters. So, brother, I am not sure why you are doing the crazy things you are doing, but it ain't cool. So, just be aware, I am watching you and I trust you won't do that again."

"Sure, Tony. Whatever you say. Uh, I'm really sorry, guy. It won't happen again."

The Ancient Paths

Tony and Rose always felt it was their responsibility to watch out for and defend their little sisters; but it seemed that they were not always able to rescue them from the clutches of their captor, Mrs. Barrett.

**

Since Rose and Karen shared a room, they always enjoyed the times when they could be together hanging out in their own room upstairs, away from the adults. They would close the door in order to keep Kevin from always running into their room and disrupting their time together. They could always find something to talk about or laugh about, as they both had imaginations as deep as the sea. On this particular day, as Anna sat on her bed, simply being quiet and playing with her dolls, Rose blurted out, "Hey, do you know who you look like?"

"Um…no."

"You look like…Bob Hope. Really!" With that, Anna burst out giggling and so did Rose. It was true. At that particular moment, the expression on Anna's face, for some reason, actually did remind Rose of Bob Hope. Anna knew that Bob Hope was a male comedian, so she really thought it was hilarious, as she actually loved Bob Hope.

Rose had a bright idea right at that moment. She was never short on brainstorms, if you can call it that. "Hey, let's do tumbles and flips on our beds. It'll be fun." Anna thought about it for a moment, then grinning, she stood up on her bed and began bouncing up and down as if the bed were a trampoline. Rose did a roll off the foot of her bed and landed on the floor. Anna giggled then tried to do a roll off her bed; however, unfortunately for her, she did not land on the floor like Rose had done. Instead, Anna's body curved to one side, and in essence what happened to her was that she landed a blow to the wall, and the dry wall caved in, leaving a small crater in the wall which Mrs. Barrett was bound to see.

Rose was scared for Anna. "Oh my gosh, Anna. What will we do?"

Anna was scared to death too, and with good reason. "I don't know, Sissy. I guess we have to tell."

"No," Rose insisted. "Let's just wait and see if she notices it first." It didn't take long though for Kevin to realize that something had happened, since he was in the next room when he heard the thuds coming from the girls' room. Upon entering the room and seeing the dent in the dry wall, Kevin turned and went directly to tell Mrs. Barrett. Within moments, Mrs. Barrett was standing in the middle of the girls' room. This was the first time Rose could recall Mrs. Barrett coming into their room since they had first arrived.

"Who did that?" Mrs. Barrett asked, pointing at the obviously busted up wall.

"I did," said Anna, timidly, as she held her head down.

Mrs. Barrett ordered Rose, "Leave the room, Rose." She all but barked the order at the girl.

Rose did not want to leave her sister in the room alone with Mrs. Barrett, but she could think of no way out of the situation for her or her sister. She simply was not big enough to be intimidating on her own, and Tony was not home at the moment. She turned and slowly walked out of the room and stood on the outside of the room looking in at her sister sitting on the bed with a very deer in the headlights expression on her face. Mrs. Barrett then grabbed the doorknob and shut the door, so that Rose was unable to see her sister at all. "God, no, please!" Rose cried. She could hear the thuds as Mrs. Barrett knocked her sister around. It made Rose crazy that she could not protect her sister from the brutal attack she knew was happening on the other side of the door. Then Rose saw Kevin peeking out from behind his and Tony's bedroom door. "I hate you, Kevin. Why did you go tell that old bitty and make her hit my sister? I didn't tell on you when you were out here naked without your stupid clothes on!"

Kevin stared after Rose as she ran down the stairs and out of the house. He knew for certain he had made an enemy of Rose. As always, Mr. Barrett was seated in his cozy spot in his easy chair, reading the paper, and only watched and listened to everything going on around him. Even though he never said a word, Mr. Barrett had no doubt about what was taking place in his home.

***

It happened again; only, this time it was a different set of circumstances. Like her sister before her, Karen still had some issues with bedwetting. She had been potty training for some time, had been weaned from diapers, but from time to time she had also been known to have an occasional bedwetting episode. Such was the case on this day. Mrs. Barrett discovered the wet spot on the bed that evening when she checked to see why Karen had not made up her bed. Mrs. Barrett called Karen to come into her room. Karen was sitting in the living room and was within hearing range of Mrs. Barrett's voice. So was Rose. Rose followed her little sister to see if she could learn what was going on. She stayed a few steps behind Karen though, in order that Mrs. Barrett would not realize she had followed her sister. When she dared to peek into Karen's room, Karen was sitting on the bed, and Mrs. Barrett stood with her belt in her hands. Rose knew what was next. She stepped into the doorway. "Please don't hit Karen. Please Mrs. Barrett." The bitter, evil old woman simply moved over to the door and closed it in Rose's face. Rose heard Karen's cries of pain as Mrs. Barrett began beating the young girl.

Rose looked around quickly, but knew that Tony was not to be found at the moment, as he was at a neighbor's house. She therefore ran into the living room and pleaded with Mr. Barrett. "Mr. Barrett, please,

please make it stop. She's hurting Karen." Rose was hysterical and crying. Without saying a word, Mr. Barrett disappeared into his room for what seemed like an eternity to Rose, then emerged and headed straight to the door of Karen's little room. He found the child on the floor crying and his wife standing over her with the belt.

When he spoke, it was in a very cool, calm, collected manner. "Karen, why don't you get up off the floor, sweetie? Go find your sisters and brother, and go outside and play."

Mrs. Barrett was incensed at her husband's intrusion into her disciplining the child. "But, David, you can't. I'm..."

"You're what, Alice? You're what? Abusing these children? Go on now, Karen. Get on out of here." With that, the small girl slowly pulled herself up off the floor, walked over to Mr. Barrett, hugged his legs and ran out of the room. He then turned his attention to his wife. "Now, Alice, you listen to me and you listen good. I love you. I have always loved you. You were so beautiful when we first met. Only, I was so in love with you, I couldn't see past the beauty of your exterior. I couldn't see how horribly ugly you really were on the inside. Then, we had our son, and he was the joy of my life. Only, when he left home at such an early age because he could not tolerate your abuse any longer, I should have stepped up to the plate and been the man I have never been, and left you then. I should have stopped the abuse before it got to that point. Then you grew old, just as I have done.

And, your true self, what is on the inside of you begun to show itself on the outside. You became as **ugly** on the outside as you were on the inside."

"Uh!" she exclaimed indignantly.

"Just shut up, Alice and listen. It's my time now. I've already called the Department of Children's Services. They will be here within the hour to pick up all of these kids. I don't know what will happen to Kevin, but the others will go back to live with their dad. Seems he's ready to take care of them now. You will never be able to take in foster children again, so there goes your extra income."

"David, you didn't."

"Yes, I did," he said in a very matter of fact voice. "I can only hope these kids will forgive me for allowing you to treat them this way. I hope I can forgive myself. If I ever, ever hear of you mistreating another child, I will deal with you personally."

"David, what are you saying?"

"I'm saying I want a divorce, Alice." With that, he headed toward the door, but he stopped inside the door frame, and without looking back, he delivered the final blow. "Oh, and by the way, Alice."

"Yes?"

"I'll see you in hell."

CHAPTER 8

Could the four children put the pain of their nightmarish existence at the Barrett's behind them? Was it possible that there could still be redemption of their tragic lives? The only accurate instrument by which to measure would be time itself.

Jose drove along a rural road while the children sat silent, as usual, with their hands folded. They had all learned that when in their father's presence, it was best to wait until spoken to before speaking— that is, everyone but Rose had learned. As usual, she was first to speak. "Where are we going this time?"

To her surprise, her dad didn't yell at her, but instead, appeared to be somewhat wistful and melancholy. "Oh, it's a surprise, Rose."

The road which wound through the rural area in the southern region of New York was lined with trees, interspersed with an occasional house. There were so many trees that if Rose hadn't known better, she would have thought they were going deep into a forest. She was beginning to wonder if they were lost.

Jose turned off the main road onto a narrow, winding gravel road which eventually came to a dead end and opened up into a huge field. To the left of them, in clear view, was a two story, gray shingled house. To the right was an old red barn, and further to the right of the barn was an old gray trailer. Jose hopped out of the car and motioned to the four children. "Come on you guys, get out."

The children were unsure of their surroundings, and as such, were slow to leave the security of the car. But, one by one, they gradually made their way out of the car onto the gravel driveway of this place which they had no clue of where it was. Full of wonder, Rose asked, "What *is* this place?"

"It's our new home. We're going to be very happy here. Just you guys wait and see." Jose sounded perhaps a bit resolute. Maybe he really did want his children to be happy. After all, it was his bribery payment to the judge and both his and his ex-wife's attorneys in Tennessee that had caused him to end up with the kids. Maybe he truly wanted to make amends for the pain and anguish he had brought on these four young, innocent lives…maybe.

Jose made his way to the front door of the house and the children followed close behind. All the children realized they were very far away from anything they had ever known in recent times, and the only familiar things to them at this point were each other and their father.

As the children filtered slowly into the house, much to their surprise, they were greeted by an attractive young lady who had shoulder length honey blond hair, and from appearances was about twenty years old. "Hello, Tony, Rose, Anna and Karen. Is that right? Did I get your names correct?" She had obviously been waiting for their arrival, but who *was* she?

Jose could see the looks of confusion on the children's faces, so he decided it was time to explain. "Guys, I want you to meet Sherry. She will be your live-in babysitter and nanny. You must be sure to mind her."

The children were bewildered. Rose realized that it had not been so very long ago when they had moved out of the slums of Binghamton, and now they were in the country, in a nice home, with a nanny no less? This just did not make sense to Rose. As usual, Rose could not help herself; she just had to open her mouth and say whatever happened to pop into her head. "But, Daddy, we're poor. How can *we* have a nanny?"

"Well, Rose, Daddy has been working very hard since you guys went into the foster home, and we are not *exactly* poor now. No, we're not *exactly* rich, but we're not *exactly* poor either. So, since I have to work so much of the time now, I needed somebody to look after you guys, and that somebody is Sherry."

Rose marveled. They had their very own nanny? How had that come about? It still didn't make sense to her.

Sherry's voice was kind and loving, something the siblings had not been used to for a very long time. Her voice carried in it an undeniable sense of comfort and compassion. Rose decided at once that Sherry must be an angel.

It was as if a light bulb had been turned on in everyone's head at the same time, and everyone, including Sherry, suddenly knew and understood their new roles. This was her first nanny job, but Sherry assumed the role of nanny with a natural ease. "Children, your rooms are upstairs. You have thirteen acres here on which to play, and you also have a creek that runs the length of the property which you can play in. I believe it's shallow enough to be safe, as long as Tony is with you when you go there. Why don't you take a look at your rooms, then go for a walk on the property and check it out before we tackle the job of putting up your belongings? I will call you in a little while when it's time to eat."

Rose couldn't contain her excitement. "Yay!" she squealed before darting up the staircase. Sherry did not have time to blink or say another word before Rose was out of her sight. Karen and Anna wasted no time in following their big sister up the staircase.

"Don't you want to see your room, Tony?" Sherry asked.

"Sure," Tony said quietly, as he stuffed his hands into his pants pockets and slowly meandered up the stairs. Sherry could see that it must be tough for Tony being the only boy.

"Look, Tony, look!" Karen squealed, if you could call it a squeal. Karen had a deep croaky voice for such a little girl. "Us girls gots a big room. You room is kinda little, Tony."

"It's okay, Karen. There are three of you and only one of me. I think Sherry's room is on the other side of your room too. And you should say 'us girls *have* a big room, Karen.'"

"But, you not a girl, Tony," Karen reasoned with him. Tony rolled his eyes at his little sister. How could he argue with that kind of logic?

"Okay, then. Let's go play," Rose interjected. She was through with the small talk. She grabbed each of her little sisters' hands and pulled them down the stairs with her. Tony was close behind. It was time to go exploring and have some fun. The children still did not know where they were, but at that moment, it did not seem to matter anymore.

The children were down the steps and flying out the front door as laughter of delight filled the air. It seemed that they had arrived. For the moment anyway, they felt *free*. The siblings ran immediately into the huge field behind the house. Since Karen was growing and was no longer a baby, instead of Tony picking Karen up and carrying her on his hip like in the old days, he grabbed her by the hand and helped her go faster, just as Rose pulled Anna along by her hand. They had never had this much room to roam around in before. At that moment, they felt for the first time in what seemed like an eternity, what it was really like to be a child. Rose was so exuberant that her eyes filled with tears.

"What's wrong, Rose?" Tony inquired of his sister.

"Nothing, I guess. I mean, this place is beautiful and all, but it just seems so strange, everything. You know, it really feels good though to be away from Mrs. Barrett and that house. She was so mean to everyone, especially Karen and Anna."

"I know, sis. I think that even Mr. Barrett finally had his fill of her. Before we left, he told me that he was moving out too."

"Right on, Mr. Barrett," was her response as she giggled and choked back more tears of joy and sadness combined.

The group of children had made their way across one huge field and now found themselves standing beside the creek that coursed through the property on which they now lived and would come to call home.

Pointing, Tony called out, "Look at that huge board over there in the rocks, Rose."

"I see that. Let's go swim in the creek, and we can lay on that board to dry off. It'll be like Gilligan's Island."

"Uh, I don't know. Maybe we should do that some other time. We don't have our clothes unpacked yet, and Sherry will be calling us for dinner in a little bit."

"Oh yeah, you're right, never mind."

There was plenty more land to be explored, and they did just that. There was wide open field after field where they could run and play chase. The children were giddy from the endorphins being released in their brains by the exercise and fresh air.

Eventually, the group began making its way back toward the direction of the house, when they heard Sherry calling them from across the field. "Hey kids! Come on back now. Time for dinner." Tony, Rose, Anna and Karen broke into a full gated run toward her voice, with Tony pulling Karen along by her hand. What a difference a day had made in the lives of the four children. Could life really be this good for them now?

***

As much as Rose loved her two younger sisters, it felt like such a tremendous load had been lifted from her when Sherry came into the picture. For starters, Rose no longer had to worry about an ugly old woman picking on her sisters when Tony wasn't around to help support her in trying to protect them. While Tony was not yet a full grown teenager, he was a fairly tall, lean young pre-teen, and while they had been at the Barrett's home, Mrs. Barrett had decided that she would limit verbal confrontations with Tony.

Rose felt assured that all was well while Sherry was with them. Sherry also did the cooking and cleaning. To Rose, it seemed a long time ago that she had been the chief cook and bottle washer of the household in the period immediately following the divorce of her parents. And most importantly, with the introduction of Sherry into their lives, their father seemed content to just let them be children without applying his brand of abuse.

***

As Sherry combed Rose's long black hair, she hummed a simple little tune. "That's pretty, Sherry. What song is that?"

"It's Amazing Grace."

"Well, I like Amazing Grace. I think I heard it in church once when I was really little." Sherry grew quiet and thoughtful. "What's wrong, Sherry?" Rose wanted to know.

"Nothing, honey. It's just that…"

"It's just that what, Sherry?"

"It's just that I haven't been to church in a very long time, and I know I should go. You all need to go to church too."

"Okay, I'll go if you want. Can Daddy go too?"

"Sure, I'll talk to your daddy soon and see if he would like for us all to go to church together." Sherry continued humming and brushing Rose's hair. "Hey, Rose. Know what?"

"No, I don't guess so, Sherry. What?"

"Well, it's just that…I love you sweetie, and I love someone else here too." Rose was tickled pink to hear Sherry say that she loved her. She had come to view Sherry as her new mother figure.

"Who else do you love, Sherry?"

"Well, I love all of you, Rose: you, your sisters and Tony. But, well, there's someone else too." Rose was not too slow, and she thought she pretty well had this one figured out, but she asked anyway.

"So, who else is there, Sherry?"

"I love someone, and his name starts with J."

Rose tried to play dumb here. "You love...my daddy?" Sherry grinned and nodded. Well, this was certainly odd. Sherry was only about...oh, TWENTY YEARS YOUNGER than Rose's dad! But, Rose loved Sherry too, and really wanted her to be a part of their family. To Rose, Sherry sort of felt like a young mommy. "That's great, Sherry! Can I tell Daddy?" Somehow, Rose thought that Sherry should have seemed happier about being in love with her dad, but Sherry looked sad when she spoke.

"No honey. No. Just let me tell him when I think it's the right time, okay? Promise me you won't say anything, Rose."

"Okay, Sherry. I promise." Maybe Sherry and their dad would get married and everything would be good, Rose thought. Maybe.

***

It was Sunday, and Rose, Tony, Karen and Anna were ready for church. "Sherry, you aren't going with us?" Rose asked.

Sherry just looked down at the floor.

"No, Rose. I'm sorry, honey. I'm going to stay here."

"Is Daddy going with us?" Jose heard his name and came out from his room, which was the only bedroom downstairs.

"No, Rose. I'm not going to church either. Mrs. Caldwell and her kids are taking you guys to church today."

The Caldwell's were the family who lived in the gray trailer. They were a slightly less fortunate family in regards to income, but they seemed to always be happy. Mr. Caldwell had been injured in a work accident years ago, but he had maintained a positive outlook on life, and so had Mrs. Caldwell. They had a son named Mark and a daughter named Thea.

"But, Sherry, I want you and Daddy to go with us."

"I know Rose, but here comes Mrs. Caldwell right now." At that very second there was a knock on the front door, and Sherry greeted Mrs. Caldwell with what was obviously a forced smile. "Good morning, Mrs. Caldwell. Thank you for taking the children today."

"Yes, thank you, Mrs. Caldwell," Jose chimed in. Rose was secretly hoping that Sherry would talk to her daddy today and tell him that she loved him! That would be a dream come true for Rose. But, Rose could never stop thinking about her own mother and wonder where she was and what she was doing.

The Ancient Paths

In Sunday school that day, Rose and the others heard the story of Jesus again, and how he had died for their sins. Rose could not understand the concept of someone dying for her sins, and neither could any of her siblings, with the possible exception of Tony. Tony was very quiet and read a lot for entertainment, so he knew a little about why it was necessary to have our sins forgiven. He always seemed to know things before Rose did. Rose knew that sin existed, but was not yet able to grasp the concept of being forgiven. Anna and Karen were just happy to hear the story of Jesus again. It made them feel good.

When the children returned home from church that day, Sherry was ironing clothes and had dinner cooking on the stove. "Why don't you children grab a piece of fruit out of the fridge, go on outside and play for a while, and I will call you when dinner is ready. We'll have an early dinner. Oh, and don't forget to change out of your church clothes before going outside."

Rose scurried up the stairs and searched for something to change into. Anna and Karen moved a little slower than Rose. Tony looked a little sullen, as he had hoped to go home and be able to read in his room. Oh well, he would take his book down to the creek side and read. Rose found one of her favorite play dresses to change into.

Once outside, Tony headed toward the creek while Rose, Anna and Karen played in the front yard by the big oak tree. Rose was humming as she skipped along then began to spin around in circles and danced around with her hands raised over her head while the ends of her dress flared out wide. She was spinning so hard that her pigtails were sticking out like propellers on a helicopter, and Anna and Karen thought their big sister was about to levitate at any moment!

"Rose, what you doing and why are you singing?" Anna asked.

Rose continued skipping and dancing, with her arms lowered. "I'm dancing."

"Why?"

"I don't really know. I don't *feel* like singing and dancing. But, I think I'm singing and dancing for God because He wants me to."

Anna looked up from the jar where she had some lightning bugs saved from the previous day. "Now you know that is perfectly ri-dic-a-lous. You making me and Karen dizzy watching you. And besides, it would help if you could sings."

Rose was very sensitive and her feelings were easily hurt. "Fine, if you don't want me to dance, I'm not going to play with you." Pouting, she stuck out her lower lip and ran down the gravel driveway.

"Wait, Rose! Don't leave us. Come back and play," Anna called after her sister, but Rose was already gone out of sight.

Where she was going, Rose hadn't a clue. She felt like hiding for some reason. She ran to the end of the driveway which was a fairly long gravel road. Then for the first time since coming to live at her new home, she noticed that there seemed to be an opening, a sort of entrance into the row of bushes at the end of the driveway. The bushes bordered the strawberry patch which was on their property. "Hmm, I wonder what's in there" Rose pondered. Looking around to make sure no one was watching her, Rose walked up to the opening in the bushes and peeked in. She had found somewhat of a tunnel inside of those bushes. She wondered how many rabbits and other wild animals had lived there before she came along. She lowered herself onto her knees and crawled into the space. She fit cozily in the opening, and she felt warm and comfortable there. "Our very own secret place," she whispered. She reached into the top of her dress and pulled out a locket, opened it up and laid it on the ground. It was the locket which with the face of Jesus in it that Miz Minnie had given her what now seemed to be so very long ago. Rose sang softly to the locket, "Jesus loves me this I know, for the Bible tells me so...." This would become her secret spot where no one knew to find her. She would tell no one of her hiding place.

***

The next morning Tony and Anna were up early, and with Karen in tow, the three of them wandered into the chicken coop section of the long red barn. "Well, Daddy usually does this, but he wants me to start doing it," Tony announced to his sisters. Chickens sitting in their respective boxes clucked away. Tony was in awe. "You know, I've never been this close to a real chicken before." He was amazed. "What do I do?"

Without hesitation, Anna scooped a hen from its perch and found its treasure. There lying in the pile of straw was a freshly laid hen egg. Anna proudly handed it to Tony, and he wrapped both hands around it. "It's still warm," he whispered. "Are we going to actually eat this?" Anna eagerly nodded consent. "Oh my," Tony said. He wasn't sure he could do that now that he knew where the eggs really came from.

Yes, at times life seemed almost normal for a change, almost.

CHAPTER 9

Rose awoke to the sound of muffled conversation coming from the direction of Sherry's room. Rose glanced at the clock. It was 12:00 a.m. Who in the world was Sherry talking to that time of night? Rose lay there a few moments thinking the talking would stop—only, it didn't. Finally, out of curiosity, Rose quietly made her way out of bed, tiptoed out of the room so as not to disturb her sisters who were sleeping soundly, and stopped in the hallway outside of Sherry's bedroom door. There was a faint glow of light seeping out from under Sherry's door, and Rose heard the voices again.

"You shouldn't be here now. This isn't right. What would the children think? You know how I feel about you, Jose.." It was Sherry's voice alright.

"What is going on in there" Rose pondered. But, then she heard the second voice.

"I don't care. I want to be here with you." It was Rose's father.

"You know how I feel about you. I love you, you know," Sherry so unpretentiously admitted. Then there was silence.

"Come on, say you love her," Rose thought to herself. But, those words never found their way to her father's lips. The only response Rose was able to discern was, "Uh huh." That was obviously not what Sherry was hoping to hear. Rose quietly stole back to her room and crawled back into bed.

***

Tony, Rose, Anna and Karen at the creek played joyfully and with that childlike abandon that people tend to forget exists. While the ripples in the water continued non-stop with their song, the children laughed and splashed each other, which really didn't matter since they were already soaked to the bone. "Let's lay out here and dry off for a while," Tony suggested.

"Okay," Anna and Karen eagerly agreed, as they sat down on the huge board of plywood which had been there since they had arrived in their new home.

"I will in a few minutes. Right now though, I'm starving,' Be right back." Rose excused herself and headed toward the house. She was as wet as a seal, but all Rose could think of was that moon pie she had seen in the kitchen that morning. She tiptoed from the front door to the kitchen, found her moon pie, inhaled it, and then opened the fridge to look for something to drink, when she noticed a faint, muffled sound. She slammed the refrigerator door and her big brown eyes scanned the surroundings to see if she could discover what the sound was. And where was Sherry? Rose followed the sound, which took her up the staircase and to the door of Sherry's room, where she found Sherry face-down on her bed, sobbing. Rose then saw that Sherry's luggage was packed and neatly lined up by her bedroom door.

"Sherry, where are you going?" Rose blurted. Before Sherry could answer, the other children were standing at the door of Sherry's room too. They had decided that they too were hungry. But, finding no Rose in the kitchen or dining room, they had followed the faint sounds of Sherry crying. Dripping wet, Rose, Anna and Karen crowded around their nanny and clung to her. Not only was Sherry their nanny, she had become their friend. Being the only guy in the group, Tony felt he could not say much, but he was pretty certain he knew what had gone down in regards to the situation at hand.

Sniffling with tears running down her cheeks and eyes red, Sherry managed to get out in broken syllables, "I'm….I'm leav…ing. Go…go..ing…..home."

Rose started crying, "Sherry, please don't go. Please don't leave us. We need you." She wrapped her arms around Sherry's neck.

"Yeah, don't leave us," Anna and Karen chimed in. They teared up and started crying too, and Tony could only look on with sorrow for Sherry, as well as for himself, and his sisters. He knew it would be bad for the four of them once Sherry left.

"Uh…uh…uh…my…old boyfriend...coming...to…get me," Sherry managed to say in between sobs. She was crying so hard it looked like she was going to break from the way her body was being racked.

The damage was done, and Rose knew it. "I love you, Sherry."

"We love you too, Sherry," Rose and Karen said simultaneously. They were so close that they seemed to operate almost like a set of twins. They moved as one.

"When are you leaving, Sherry?" Rose asked.

"Tomorrow," Sherry responded.

"Oh, why so soon?"

"Because, sweetie, it's just time for me to go, as much as I hate to. I will miss you all."

***

The next day, all the children followed Sherry out to the driveway, and when the white car pulled up and the handsome young man got out and helped Sherry get her baggage into the trunk of the car, Rose felt her heart sink. Sherry had been their reprieve from a life of uncertainty and mental and emotional abuse. What were they going to do now? Their young, worried faces said it all. They were losing their nanny and their friend. Rose and Tony both worried about what would happen to their younger sisters without Sherry.

"You children behave. I'm going to miss you all." Each of the children took turns hugging Sherry good-bye.

When it was Rose's turn, she could not hide her sense of loss at the departure of her beloved nanny. "Sherry, I love you. Please don't leave us."

Sherry could hardly hold back the tears. "I'm sorry, sweetie. You guys deserve to have someone in your life who will love you and take care of you. But, I have to go. My part in your life is over now. I pray that someone else who cares about you all and loves you will be sent into your life. I love you, Rose." She kissed Rose on the top of her head, hopped into the car along with the nameless young man, and the four children were left staring after the car, as dust filled the air. Sherry was gone from their sight and from their lives, forever, just like that.

***

Before Sherry had actually left, Rose had already begun to grieve the loss of her in their lives, the only mother image she and her siblings had had in their lives in recent times. The day after Sherry left, Rose stole away and made her way down the steps which led from the kitchen into the basement. The basement was dark and damp, with nothing more than dirt for a floor. The walls were made from huge rocks which jutted out and left no illusion of refinement or remodeling. Rose sat on the wooden bench, the only chair in the whole basement, looked forlornly at the walls of the dark, depressing room and began to cry.

The poor girl was so grief-stricken that she didn't notice the sound of footsteps right away, but then the sound got closer, and Rose realized that someone else was in the room with her. Tony emerged from the shadow of the stairwell. He came and sat down beside her. He was very concerned about his sister. "What are you doing down here all by yourself?"

Rose turned to her brother in despair. "Tony, I just don't know how to say what I feel. I'm not good with words like you, but I'm real sad that Sherry left. I'm afraid of Daddy, and I feel all alone." She started to cry again, and her big brother put a comforting arm around her shoulder.

Chuckling, Tony told her, "First of all, let me say that no one, I mean no one is better with words that you Rose!" She sniffled, looked at her brother through her tears and had to laugh just a little bit. She understood what he meant. She knew that Tony thought she talked too much. "Secondly, you still have me, Rose. And you have Anna and Karen. We're all here and in this together, whether we like it or not." So many things which Rose had held back for so long suddenly welled up inside her and gushed forth from her innermost being, as she sat there in the cool, dark, damp basement that afternoon and wept on her brother's shoulder.

It's strange how sometimes our childhood can be stolen from us, just like that. But, then again it could be that their childhood had been stolen a long time ago.

***

In the months that followed after Sherry had taken her leave of the family, a rapid succession of nannies passed through the lives of the four children. Each one was young and mostly inexperienced at being a nanny. The last young woman who came to stay with the family stayed a short while, only to end up pregnant, and moved back home to her parents. Whose baby she was carrying, Rose was never certain of.

The day finally came when Jose informed his children, "Guys, I am tired of paying nannies who are no good at the job. You guys are going to have to take care of yourself. Tony and Rose, you are big kids now, so you can look after your sisters."

Rose couldn't help but ponder whether it was the nannies that were no good, or if it was her daddy who was simply running off what had become a long procession of young women who had attempted unsuccessfully to fill Sherry's shoes. Rose was not too knowledgeable about the ways of the world; however, she had heard talk in school about sex and what it meant. She was a little more than certain that her father had been having sex with all the nannies he had hired, especially Donna, the one who had turned up pregnant and moved back home with her parents. The only discrepancy with the theory was that Donna may have already been pregnant when she moved in. Rose just never knew.

Rose often wondered if her mother was still in Tennessee and how she was doing. She also wondered if her mother knew where they were. Even the seeming beauty of what had been their "new life" had become marred and was a foreshadowing of what would become a much greater darkness than any of the children would ever have imagined possible.

CHAPTER 10

As had become tradition, the children were outside playing after dinner. Rose was dancing and singing while Anna and Karen were busy looking for fireflies. Tony sat under the oak tree reading a book. Suddenly, the magic of twilight play was shattered by a voice from another world. "Rose! Come here, right now!" Rose froze in her tracks and looked helplessly at her brother, as if asking him what she should do. Tony quietly nodded at her, signaling that she should go on and see what their father was wanting with her. She sucked in her breath, counting to ten very quickly. She then headed for the house.

Once inside the house, Rose found her father leaning against the kitchen counter with one hand, and with the other hand holding half a loaf of French bread. She entered the room and approached her father with her head held low and a finger in her mouth. "Yes, sir?" she spoke quietly.

While Rose was timid, innocent and scared, fire flashed from her father's eyes as he gritted his teeth and angrily shook the loaf of bread at her. "Who threw this in the garbage? Do you know? Who?"

She held her head even lower and stared at the ground. "I did, sir."

94

The Ancient Paths

Jose shook the loaf of bread even harder at the girl. "Why? Why did you do that? I work hard to buy food for you, and you repay me by throwing food away!"

Rose tried to defend herself. "But it was stale, really dry and hard."

Jose raged at the girl like a mad man. "I don't care for your excuses. If you think it is so easy to throw bread away, I will show you." He was now shouting at her. "Here, eat every last bite of it." He shoved the bread at Rose as she stared at him in disbelief and horror. He forced her to take the loaf of bread. "I said take it."

Rose slowly lifted her hand and took the loaf of bread from her father, as tears spilled out from the corners of her eyes. She could barely find her voice, and when she spoke, it was in a whispered voice. "But, Daddy, it's been in the garbage."

Jose was unrelenting. "I don't care. Now eat it."

Rose slowly put the loaf of stale bread to her mouth and began to eat it, as tears continued to fall to her cheeks.

***

That night, as the children gathered together and lined up on their knees to say their prayers in Sherry's old room, Rose couldn't help herself. She spoke what was on her mind as she prayed. "Dear Lord, I know this may be wrong, but please, please just take my daddy so I won't have to kill him." In shock, all of her siblings dropped their hands from the prayer position and looked at her.

Against his own will, Tony tried to be the voice of reason. "Rose, I know that Daddy makes us all feel like…well, like we all want to kill him sometime, but we really shouldn't pray like that."

"I know, Tony. I won't do it again…I guess."

Tony and his father had not had any confrontations since Tony had been a toddler. Tony was concerned about what he had observed to be his father's abusive treatment of the opposite sex, but the young man knew he was helpless to do anything about it, as he was only eleven and a half years old, and was no match for his father's aggressive, abusive, brute physical strength.

Yet, there were moments of happiness for the four children. Yes, there were fleeting moments, as it were, when the children could truly be children, and not feel as though they were prisoners of war in a prison camp. On those days when it was beautiful outdoors on the weekend, the children would try to stay outside and play. None of them dared to cross their father's path, if it were not absolutely necessary. Oftentimes they would go down to the creek and wade in the swiftly running water. Sometimes they would even imagine that their large piece of plywood was actually a raft and that they could float away from their father and his house forever. Sometimes they would imagine that they were at the old homestead in Hickman County. They had memories of the place from their very early childhood.

In the evenings, when the sun began to set, they would play hide-and-go-seek or blind man's bluff. Anna and Karen would even make dolls for themselves from the stems of dandelions. In the twilight, were some of those very special times when they would truly remember they were still children, and not senior citizens.

However, in between those few, brief happy moments of their childhood, the storm raged on. It seemed as though Jose became more bitter and much quicker to resort to anger and violence in those days, but the atrocities against the four young, innocent children did not stop there.

***

"Daddy, my tooth still hurts," Rose complained on Monday morning, as she rubbed her swollen jaw.

"I know, Rose. I'm staying home from work tomorrow to take you to the dentist. I've already made the appointment."

Rose cringed. "But, I thought your friend Alice was going to take me."

"Nope, I am." Rose was scared to death of her father, and with good cause.

The following morning, after Tony, Anna and Karen left for school, Rose sat silently waiting for her father to take her to the dentist. Finally, she grew anxious and tired of waiting. "Are you ready to go now, Daddy?"

Even though Rose was only a child, she recognized that the look in her father's eyes was one of a deranged madman. She had accepted that knowledge long ago, that her father was not normal. He did not answer her right away, but would only glare at her with that glassy-eyed insane look of his. "Oh my God," she thought to herself. "What did I do wrong this time?" She knew he was capable of extremely cruel actions at any moment.

"Do you want to…fool around before we go?" He asked his daughter. Rose began to panic and was terror stricken. She knew what he meant by that. It would not be the first time her father had targeted his oldest daughter for his deviant sexual behavior. Her mind raced back to a time in the past when she had spent the night with her father during court ordered visitation during her parents' divorce. Rose always knew what had happened that night was wrong, wrong, wrong.

She wished so badly that she could say she loved her father in the way that her friends at school loved their dads, but it would not have been the truth.

Suddenly Rose blurted out, "No! I don't! Leave me alone!" She tried to run, but her father would not let her escape. She reached the front door and turned the knob, only to find that her father had locked the door and removed the key which was always in the lock. Her father grabbed her by her braids and slapped her. In spite of her screaming, kicking, hitting and refusal to comply with her father, he forced himself on the terrified girl yet again.

"And don't forget, young lady, you had better not tell anyone. It could be very bad for all of us if you do."

"God, can this really be my father?" Rose's mind raced as she wondered to herself, "Who *is* my father, really? This **cannot** be *my* father! This is the Devil!"

Sobbing when it was over, Rose jumped up and ran to the bathroom where she felt so ashamed, so badly about herself and so dirty that all the poor girl could do was cry. After she had heard about this in school, it confirmed for her what she had already known, this was not meant to be something that happened between a father and daughter. This was reserved for relationships between two grown, consenting adults. "God, please forgive me, but I really hate my father," Rose wept in the bathroom. Who else could she turn to in this difficult, dark moment? But she found herself wondering, did God ***really*** hear her?

Rose was growing to hate herself for something which she could in no way control. She was losing all hope of ever having a normal life. She even began to wonder if she had faith in anything anymore. She no longer danced and sang for the Lord. And not only that, where was her mother, she wondered. Goodness, how she missed her mom. Rose felt so old now, but she was only nine and a half years old. She had to keep herself in check, as she did not want her brother and sisters to know what was happening to her. She was not sure exactly what would happen to all of them if she were to tell, but she was afraid to take that chance and find out. They all lived by the mighty hand of justice which their father doled out at his discretion, and she was concerned for her younger sisters too. What was her father doing to her sisters? She had to wonder. She also had to wonder how long Tony would be safe from their father's wrath. She had a very bad feeling about that when she would stop to consider what the possibilities were.

Jose had no rhyme or reason to his brutalizing, belittling, demeaning behavior he displayed toward his children. One day it might be Rose, one day it might be Anna, one day it was Karen's turn to be picked on. The children lived in constant fear and walked through life as though they were walking on eggshells. Tony had to helplessly stand by and know that there was nothing he could do to save his sisters.

***

The day came when time finally ran out for Tony. He was for the most part a quiet, reflective young man who never gave his father a moment of trouble. Tony always cared for his sisters and tried his best to help keep things together in the family. He was the kind of son any parent would have been proud of. He was studious and did well in school. But, was that enough for his father? It would appear that it was not.

It was Saturday and all was quiet at home. Tony lay in his room on the bed reading a James Bond book, while Rose, Anna and Karen sat in the living room downstairs watching television. So, it was the three girls who were present when a knock was heard at the front door. Jose hurried to the door and greeted his company. "Hello, Mr. Davis, Mrs. Davis and Elizabeth. So good to see you again."

Rose wondered to herself, "Who are these people? And, how does our dad know them? We've never heard of them before."

Mr. Davis shook hands with Jose. "Good afternoon, Mr. Rivera. Are these your lovely daughters?"

"Yes, meet Rose, Anna and Karen."

Mr. Davis smiled at the girls and asked, "How do you do, Rose,

Anna and Karen? It's very nice to meet all of you." But, the sisters were only able to respond by staring blankly at the guests. It would have been difficult for Mr. and Mrs. Davis not to notice that the girls were apparently afraid to speak.

Jose broke the momentary silence. "Please, Mr. Davis, won't you and your family please come in and sit down." He very gallantly held his hand out and motioned for them to enter the living room. He then turned and looked questioningly at Rose. "Where is your brother, Rose?" he asked in a very matter of fact fashion. It was more of a statement than a question.

Rose felt like this had to be another trick question of his, so she timidly responded, "I don't know." Her father clinched his teeth in that way that only he had of doing which could make his children cringe and want to run and hide somewhere. He headed for the staircase and took the stairs two at a time. At the top of the stairs was Tony's room. There lying on his bed, in his quiet manner, reading a book was Tony.

But, Jose began to yell at the boy, "What the heck are you doing up here? Don't you know we have company? Quit reading that trash!" With that, Jose, with almost superhuman speed, removed his belt and began to beat Tony with it. Jose hit Tony hard enough that Tony came up off the bed trying to escape the belt, and when he did, Jose began to kick him and kick him. He kicked his son all the way down the steps. Tony hit the floor at the bottom of the stairs with a loud thud. Rose was standing in the dining room when Tony landed at the bottom of the stairs and ran out the front door weeping and wailing. Everything happened so suddenly that Rose thought she was seeing things when her brother landed on the floor and then ran out the door. It was like something out of a nightmare.

In the living room, Mrs. Davis looked at her daughter and could see the look of fear on her face. So, Mrs. Davis decided to speak up. "George, let's go. I don't want to be here another minute." He opened his mouth as if to protest, but then changed his mind. He could tell that his wife was serious.

"Yes, dear. Let's go." He led his family back into the dining area which was the centrally located room one must pass through either coming to or leaving the house. Jose had returned from upstairs where he had just brutalized his son for reading a book while there was company in the house. George approached Jose, "Mr. Rivera, we'll come back some other time."

"No, please stay," Jose tried to insist, but his visitors had already seen enough.

"No, we'll just leave. Take care." George shook Jose's hand and held his breath. He did not know what to say about the scene he and his family had just witnessed.

Once the Davis family was inside the car, Mrs. Davis was the first to speak. "That was horrible. I can't believe someone would do such a thing to their own child, *especially* with company in the house. Who does that?"

George took a deep breath and looked his wife squarely in the face. "Miriam, listen. You must promise me you will not get involved in this."

"How can I promise to do that, George? Are you kidding me? Didn't you see what was going on there? Those girls were scared to death to even talk, and your friend kicked the son down the stairs. Somebody needs to know what's going on here!"

"No," George persisted. "I have to work with that man, and he carries a lot of clout at the plant. Just let it go. We are to forget we were even here today. Do you understand?" Miriam stared holes through her husband, saying nothing, but she understood the significance of his words. Jose outranked her husband, and he could make trouble for him at work. She nodded reluctantly, as she realized, as did her husband, that the specter of those four children would haunt them for a long time. But, this scene today was a secret that would go to the grave with them and their daughter. After all, it was 1966 and people just didn't talk about those things in those days. And with that, they left, without ever trying to help the four children, and they never came back.

CHAPTER 11

Somewhere, in the deep south in Tennessee, Leroy, Emma and Clarence sat quietly sipping coffee as the soft tick-tock of the cuckoo clock filled the still air of the room. The family had moved out of Hickman County long ago and now lived in Nashville. Margie meandered into the room looking tired and worn. She poured herself a cup of coffee and joined the others at the table. Leroy could see the look of exhaustion on his sister's face. He knew her nerves had been frayed and worn ever since Jose had disappeared into the night with her children and with his other "family."

Being the wonderful, caring big brother that he was, Leroy placed a comforting hand over his sister's hand. Margie, looking defeated, yet defiant, said, "Okay. Here it is. It's been too long since he took my babies and left here with them. I know that Edwina and her kids came back here months ago. She made sure she got her kids out of there, and then she left mine, with that...that monster! I've checked. He's already moved and left no forwarding address. Not only that, he's changed jobs. There's no trace of him. How do I know that he hasn't done something horrible to my children, just so that I can't be with them? How do I know that he hasn't even killed them? Somebody tell me, won't you? How do I know?"

Margie was starting to break down. She sobbed so hard that her body was almost in convulsions. Emma could hardly stand to see her oldest daughter so torn up.

However, Leroy had a ray of hope to offer to his sister. "Sis, listen to me. I have a friend, a detective, who thinks he might be able to help."

CHAPTER 12

Rose awoke trembling that morning. Anna and Karen were already awake and were sitting in their beds looking at their older sister, waiting for her to wake up. When Rose realized that her two little sisters were looking at her when she woke up, she was actually very glad to see them. "Hi, guys. What's going on?"

Anna responded, "Nothing. We just waiting for you to wake up. It's Saturday and we want you to fix us something to eat."

"Okay, in just a minute, but first I wanted to tell you guys that I had a really, really weird dream last night."

"Ooh," Karen almost whispered. "What happened in your dream, Sissy?"

Rose gave her account of the dream. "Well, I don't really understand the whole thing, but in the dream, Daddy was dressed up in his Air Force uniform again. He was getting ready to go to a meeting. Out of nowhere, there was this…this thing, sort of like a ghost or a spirit that appeared. It scared us all to death. Karen, you could say something, some magical word that would make the ghost disappear. We all tried to stand close to you so that we would be safe. We started crying and saying, 'Daddy, Daddy, don't leave us. Take us with you.' But he would only say, 'Children, I have to go. I must leave, but I will be back.' He left us, and in my dream, I became so nervous, so scared, that I left you all, and I walked to the other side of the big hill here behind our house. I could see the sun setting over that hill when I walked away. I was gone for a year. When I came back though, the spirit had killed all of you."

She looked at her siblings, as if seeking an explanation that would give her the answer as to the significance of her dream. "Well, I don't understand that, so don't look at me, Sissy," Anna exclaimed as she shook her head in bewilderment.

"I don't know, but I'm glad I was the one that could scare the ghost away," Karen chimed in as she clapped her little hands.

Rose shook her head, rolled her eyes and had to grin. She loved her little sisters, and she did know that they would be too young to understand or explain her dream to her, but she was glad she had them to tell.

In the next room, Tony was just waking up. His eyes were immediately wide open instead of opening slowly as he usually did in the mornings. He hopped out of bed, and as he reached his hand behind him, he had the shocking realization that his pajamas were wet.

"Oh man. Dad hates this stuff."

Hoping that he could throw his father off his trail, Tony quickly pulled off his wet pajamas and put on something dry. He took the wet bedclothes off the bed and shoved them in his closet. He then pulled the bedspread up, took a deep breath and headed down the stairs, where Jose happened to be sitting in the dining room, reading a paper and sipping on his morning coffee.

"Good morning, sleepyhead," Jose chuckled. He was attempting to be good natured on this beautiful morning. "Why don't you guys go for a walk today and get some exercise."

"Uh, okay, dad. Sure thing. Umm, let us eat some breakfast, then we'll get ready and we'll be out of here for a while." Tony tried really hard to be cool. He was afraid his father would take one look at him and be able to tell what had happened. It was as though none of them could have a thought that was private, as Jose always knew their thoughts, or so it seemed.

***

That morning, after breakfast, Tony, Rose, Anna and Karen left their father in the dining room to study his electronics books, and they were off on their hike. The weather had started to cool off somewhat and it was not quite as much fun to go out walking as it had been even a month earlier. They weren't exactly wild about the idea of going out for a walk in that climate; and yet, it was better than having to sit in the house with their father all day and be confined to their rooms, and having to talk in whispered hushes so as not to bother their father while he studied. They didn't understand why he was always studying anyway. What was he studying for? He was an electronics engineer. Maybe he was having to study to keep up on advances in technology. Who knew?

"Well, where are we walking to anyway?" Rose asked Tony once they were all outside the house.

"I don't know," he admitted. He took a quick survey of their surroundings to see if there was anything that they had *not* already explored. He pointed in the direction of the big hill behind their house. There were also railroad tracks which ran along the side of the hill. The children had never been beyond the railroad tracks.

"Ooh. That would be fun, I guess. Do you think we can make that?" Rose inquired.

Anna, who always seemed to have some unexplainable insight or wisdom for her young age said, "Of course we can. We're kids." Tony and Rose had to laugh at her. She was right. They were kids, and they could do this.

The foursome headed in the direction of the train track and hoped for the best. They waited and looked in both directions to make sure that nothing was coming down the tracks. Once they were sure, they crossed the tracks and began their long ascent up the side of the hill, which was actually a small mountain. They lived in southern New York, on the New York side of the northern mountains of Pennsylvania. The hill was steeper than Tony had ever imagined it could be.

Leaves had fallen within recent weeks, so the ground was covered in those richly colored leaves of fall. The winds howled around them, and their jackets and gloves did not seem quite sufficient for the weather, but they pressed on anyway. In recent weeks, they had been allowed to get a dog which Anna named Daniel. Daniel was the fifth wheel on this expedition and basically led the way for everyone else, since it was easier for him to scale the side of the mountain.

Even though the wind was high and did howl frequently, there was plenty of sunlight which streamed through the multicolored leaves, making the walk even more beautiful. The children felt as though they had actually transcended to some higher level in a spiritual sense, not just a physical sense. Wherever they were, it was some place quite different from anything or any other place they had ever seen before. Occasionally, they would spot an isolated house through the trees, but never did see any human being when they were hiking.

Karen still had the shortest legs of all, and as such, she was the first to tire out. "I'm really tired, Tony," she panted.

"I know, Sis. Here, let me carry you."

"I'm too big now, Tony. You can't carry me anymore."

"Well, I might not be able to carry you, but I can give you a ride on my shoulders. You're still short enough that you can ride on them." So, Karen agreed and climbed onto Tony's shoulders with help from her sisters when Tony squatted down to her level. Daniel was patient and would stop every time the children did.

Karen was happy now, and Rose held Anna's hand to make sure she did not fall behind. Anna had been having trouble with her hip recently, so Rose knew that Anna was not exactly comfortable on the walk either, but they were having fun.

When the children finally came to a place where the ground leveled off, they were able to make out a blur of some images in the distance through the trees, however they were not certain of what they were seeing. Tony turned to Rose and Anna, "Do you see that?" he asked as he pointed straight ahead.

"Yes, I do," said Rose. Anna nodded her head in agreement.

"Well, what is it?" Tony asked them.

Anna spoke up, "I don't know, but we're here, so let's find out." It seemed that there was not much she was afraid of, so the siblings all continued forward. As they drew nearer to the blurred image, they saw an undetermined number of deer running through the woods. Where the sunlight met the leaves, a prism of color filtered through and it became apparent that what they had found was in fact an old, deserted grave yard. On one headstone was written, "Choose wisely the path you will travel, and always remember: 'For He shall give his angels charge over thee, to keep thee in all thy ways'."

"Oh my gosh," were the only words Rose could manage to get out. "Tony, what does that mean?"

"It's from Psalm 91. Psalm 91:11, to be exact," he spoke, barely above a whisper. "The prayer of protection. I remember it from Sunday school. 'He that dwelleth in the secret place of the most High shall abide under the shadow of the Almighty.'"

"I have never been to a graveyard before." Rose seemed to be in a trance. "Is this a real graveyard, Tony?"

"Well, by the looks of this place, I would say that it would appear so," he affirmed.

Karen, in her little girl manner of unpretentiousness asked, "Is this where Daddy is going to bury us?"

That brought Rose back to reality. Chills ran down her spine. She had never verbalized that thought, but she had wondered often, if she had thoughts of killing her own father, did her father maybe also have thoughts of killing her or any of her siblings? She couldn't help but think about that sometimes. Yet, she spoke in a reassuring manner to her little sister, "Shhh. We shouldn't think or say those kinds of things, Karen. Daddy is not going to hurt us." However, even Rose knew it was a lie when she said it, and she was sure that Karen knew that too.

Tony turned to their guide, "Daniel, let's go home."

"Yeah," interjected Anna. "The only path I'm interested in is the path out of here. Lead the way, Daniel." She sounded so mature all of a sudden.

Daniel put his nose to the ground and began to sniff in order to smell their tracks from the journey there, and sure enough, he headed back in the direction of home. One by one, the children fell in line to follow their dog. Rose was the last to follow, but as she turned to leave, she thought she saw someone or something move among the trees. She quickly looked around in all directions to be sure of what it was she thought she had seen, but saw nothing. She could not, however, quite shake the feeling that they had not been alone in that beautiful, yet isolated place. Was it just another deer? Was it a rabbit? Perhaps, but for the moment, she realized that the others were far ahead of her by then, and she must hurry to catch up.

The Ancient Paths

Right before sundown, the children arrived back home. They all wondered where they had actually been that day, and even more, how they had managed to make it back. "Daniel must have some blood hound in him, you guys," Karen so astutely reasoned.

Jose sat exactly where the children had left him hours earlier, at the dining room table reading an electronics magazine entitled *Electronics*. "So, how was your walk?" he inquired of the children.

In unison, all the children responded, "Fine, sir." And with that, the girls scurried up the stairs before he had a chance to say anything else.

Tony, too, had turned to leave the room, but Jose stopped him. "Tony, wait a minute." Tony stopped dead in his tracks. He seemed frozen in place, unable to turn around and look at his father.

Jose stepped out of the room for a brief moment. When he returned, he was holding Tony's bed sheets in his hand. Tony still had not turned around to face his father, but now Jose ordered him to do so. "Turn around, son."

Tony knew he had better obey. He exhaled slowly and turned around, only to see his father holding the sheets up high in the air. Jose glared at his son. Tony winced under his breath.

"What is this?" Jose asked the obvious.

The Ancient Paths

Tony wasn't trying to be cocky, but he simply did not know how to answer his father, as he knew Jose had apparently already made up his mind that Tony had committed a felony of some sort. Jose knew that from time to time Tony had a problem controlling his bladder, but did nothing to help the poor lad cope with the problem. Instead, he had a way of making the situation much worse. "It looks like my sheet, sir," answered Tony finally.

"What was it doing in your closet?"

"Well, I woke up and um...I had had an accident."

Jose threw the sheet down only to reveal that underneath the sheet in his hand was a wooden stick covered in leather, which was essentially the same thing as a horse whip. "Come over here," he ordered Tony.

Tony closed his eyes, as if to muster up his courage, took a deep breath and obediently went to his father.

With one hand, Jose grabbed Tony by the arm, and with his other hand held high up over his head, he brought the leather covered stick down sharply and struck Tony over and over and over. With each whack of the stick against his back and his bottom, Tony gritted his teeth to try and bear the force of the blow, but it was finally too much and he had to let out the screams from the pain. The boy was beaten so severely he could hardly stand.

When Jose finally let go of Tony's arm, he gave him the order, "Now go to your room. No, better yet, you sleep in the garage tonight." The garage was in fact nothing more than the barn, which had no door or heat in it, and the temperature was getting colder now that the sun had gone down.

Rose, Anna and Karen, horrified, had been standing at the stop of the stairs and had listened to their brother yelling in pain from the beating he received. "Poor Tony, he can't help it," Rose whined. She felt so helpless to do anything to help any of them. She felt certain that she and her brother must feel the same way about their situation. Was there no one who could help them?

Karen whispered softly to Rose, "Sissy?"

"Yeah?"

"I hate Daddy."

Anna's eyes narrowed as she agreed with her little sister. "Me too, Karen."

That day, when the Caldwell's heard the screams coming from the Rivera home, they chose to ignore them. Even though they were aware that some things which did not appear to be exactly kosher were going on next door at the Rivera's, they dared not rock the boat. After all, they rented the land that their trailer was on from Jose. They didn't want to risk losing their home.

***

A week had passed and Tony was still sleeping in the garage. He lay on a cot and was covered by nothing more than an old army blanket. Except for his rust colored companion Daniel, he was all alone. He leaned over the side of the cot, petted his little friend, then picked him up. "Good night, Daniel. At least I have you." Daniel happily wagged his tail and curled up into a little ball under the covers with Tony which helped to keep Tony warmer. It was, after all, now below freezing in the southern region of New York every night.

That night, Rose, Anna and Karen stood in Tony's room staring out of the second story window in the direction of the barn. All of the children were beginning to wise up to the fact that if they did not begin to speak up and take some form of action, they were doomed to be slaves to their father's endless reservoir of abuse. While they could not overpower him with physical strength, they could unite in spirit and maybe, just maybe, they could become more of a deterrent against their father's abuse.

Anna had had enough. "I'm tired of Daddy making Tony sleep out there. And, it's cold. That's so mean." She defiantly unlocked the window in Tony's room.

From the garage Tony could see the shadows of the girls against the light coming from his room. He looked up from his cot and saw that Anna was unlocking the window. She pulled up the window and waved at Tony. When he rose from his cot in the barn and stepped into the driveway, Anna motioned for him to come in through the window. Being young and agile, Tony was able to scale the side of the house without too much difficulty, make his way to the roof outside his window and into his room. The girls all hugged him at once. "You don't need to stay out there anymore, Tony," Anna said.

Rose had to admire her sister's spunk. Anna had defied their father and done what she knew was the right thing to do. Rose had never realized until now that both of her sisters were turning into rather big girls nowadays, and Tony never did sleep in the garage again either.

■■■

CHAPTER 13

Was there no one who could help the children? Many was the night when Rose would go to bed and lie awake for hours contemplating, "How could I kill Daddy without anyone knowing who did it? Would that be possible?" But, try as she may, she could not figure out a way to rid herself and her siblings of their father without being found out. What a sad indictment that such a young and innocent child would be driven to have thoughts of killing her own father.

So many of the things which the children endured while living with their sociopathic father were insane, inhuman and sadistic. How could any child be normal, or even have normal thoughts, after being exposed to such a harsh, domineering and abusive upbringing? At times, it was against all odds that the children would even be able get up in the mornings and try to carry on. Despair and hopelessness were their constant companions. One of the many difficulties in living with a father who was deranged, was that the children never knew which personality he would display from day to day. He could change as quickly as a chameleon. Just when they knew they hated him the most, sometimes he would surprise them yet again.

As Tony lay in his bed sleeping soundly, his father came into the room and stood staring at his son. For a brief moment, he looked as if he would go into one of his rages again, but just as quickly, he seemed to change his mind. He shook Tony gently. Tony rolled over, rubbed his eyes and looked at his father through the morning cobwebs which had not had time to clear. Jose hesitated, then spoke as if he was the most sensitive, thoughtful father in the world. "Son, I was thinking. How would you guys like to go skating tonight after we get through washing clothes at the Laundromat in town?"

Tony's eyes had finally opened all the way. He looked tired and worn to be so young. "Sure, Daddy. That would be great."

That night at the skating rink, Rose skated happily around the rink as Anna and Karen lagged behind, trying to help each other stay up on their skates. Tony passed them all, skating backwards and waving as he passed them by. From somewhere in the skating rink, a little girl named Monica, who was a school friend of Rose's, appeared and grabbed Rose's hand. Together they skated with hands locked as Jose sat on a bench at the edge of the ice and carefully observed his children. To the average bystander, Jose appeared to be nothing more than a concerned, involved parent.

The following day was the weekend once again, but Jose had to work, which was a little unusual for a Saturday; but the children were left to look after themselves and do chores. Rose carefully removed some of the folded tee shirts and socks from the basket of recently laundered clothes and took them to her father's room. As she placed her father's socks inside the sock drawer, she noticed the corner of a clear plastic bag, which turned out to be nothing more than a bag of unopened Hershey's Kisses. "Oh my," she thought, "I would love to have one of those. Daddy would have a cow though." She closed the drawer, started to step away, but seemed unable to make herself move.

The thought of those Kisses was so enticing. They were rarely ever given candy, and to discover that her father had a whole stash of chocolate hidden away for himself was a bit of a shock for Rose, but not completely. "It's just not fair," she reasoned with herself. Try as she might to walk away from the temptation and allure of the newly wrapped, unopened pieces of inviting chocolate, she couldn't. She carefully looked around to make certain no one was going to walk in on her; she quietly opened the drawer again, and practically drooled when she imagined the taste of the chocolate melting in her mouth. It had been so long since she had been allowed to eat candy. She finally decided the thing to do was to open a small hole in the corner of the bag. After doing that, she removed a handful of the candy, slid the bag to the bottom of the socks, then carefully and slowly closed the drawer.

Muttering to herself, she said, "I don't know if this is worth it not. I'm sure it's just a matter of time before Daddy sees that, but it's too late now."

The Ancient Paths

One week later, after dinner that evening, as the children played in their rooms, Jose stood in the dining room with his hands on his hips and with a look on his face that could kill. He opened the door at the bottom of the staircase and yelled, "Tony! Rose! Get down here, right now!" Immediately the feet of the two were pounding on the stairs and they appeared before their father.

They stood at attention and spoke in unison, as if being called to formation in the military, "Yes, sir?"

Jose reached to the table behind him and produced the bag of chocolates that had been opened and partially eaten. Rose had given in to the temptation to make several clandestine trips back to the secret bag of chocolates. Once she had gotten started, she had not been able to stop, so the bag was now much closer to being empty than it had been initially. Jose was so angry that he was trembling. "Which of you did…this?"

Since Tony was innocent, he had no problem with speaking up first and admitting, "I didn't."

Try as she may, Rose wanted to speak up and admit her guilt, but she was scared to death. "I didn't," she lied.

As was his custom when he was upset, Jose's eyes were now bulging in his head; then with lightning speed, he produced his razor strap belt and stood, glaring and clinching his teeth. "I am going to beat the truth out of you two."

Rose was horrified. First, she witnessed Jose thrash Tony on the seat of his pants, and Tony yelled out from the pain. Next, Jose turned to Rose, grabbed her arm and unleashed the full fury of his wrath with that belt. She tried to protect her bottom by putting her hands over it. She cried out loud and winced from the pain, "Stop, Daddy, stop!" Her father then turned back to Tony and struck him even harder. All Tony could do was let out a horrible yell.

Something within Rose snapped as she watched her brother taking the punishment for something she knew she had done. She knew her brother suffered much pain at the hand of their father already. She could not stand to see this go on any longer. She would not let her brother pay for her crime. "Stop it! I did it! Tony didn't do it! It was me! I'm sorry!" She was hysterical and sobbing. "I ate the candy. Don't spank Tony, please. I'm sorry, Tony. Please forgive me."

Her tears had no effect on her father's emotions. His expression become one of pure rage. As if it would make amends for what he had done to his son, he handed what was left of the bag of chocolates to Tony. "Here, you can have these." Tony numbly accepted the candy. Jose turned to Rose and shook the razor strap belt at her. "And you!" was all he said. Without uttering another word, he grabbed her by the arm again, and the belt came down on her bottom over and over and over and over. He had become like a man possessed.

Tony suddenly stepped forward and spoke up, "Daddy, stop it! You're killing Rose!"

Jose had been so enraged that he had not realized Rose had become limp and was no longer conscious. As the realization dawned on him, he finally stopped his assault on the girl. "Oh my God. What have I done?" He had been holding her by the arm and beating her while she was already unconscious. He let go of her arm, the belt still clutched in his hand, and stood staring at the crumpled heap on the floor.

Rose was not dead, but severely beaten and traumatized, all in the name of punishment for eating some chocolate, and being too afraid to admit to it. She had known that her father would beat her regardless.

That night, as Rose lay in her bed in a deep sleep, and Anna and Karen were asleep in their beds, a hand shook Rose and caused her to stir from her slumber. Tony whispered softly, "Rose, come on, wake up. You have to wake up."

She opened her eyes and whimpered, "I'm sorry, Bubba. I shouldn't have let that happen to you."

Tony reassured her, "Shh. Quiet now. That's okay. Rose, we've got to get out of here before it is too late for all of us. Daddy almost killed you tonight. I think he's really a little bit crazy."

"But, Tony, I don't think I can make it. It hurts too bad to move."

"Well, you guys stay here. I'm going to try to go get us some help," he would not be deterred from doing something to change their plight.

"Be careful, please, Tony."

He nodded his head then tiptoed back into his room. Once in his room, he raised his window very slowly, so as not to make too much noise, then he climbed onto the roof. Once he was on the roof, Tony grabbed the ledge and eased himself down, dropped to the ground and took off running. Where he was going, he wasn't sure. He knew he could not go to the Caldwell's for help. They would just wake up his dad and tell him everything. They were too afraid of losing their rental property! "I know," he thought, "I'll go to John's home and call the police. He just lives about a half mile down the main drive." Tony had become very close with a young man from school named John, and John was at least aware of Tony's father's abuse. "John and his parents will know what to do," Tony thought out loud, as he ran for all it was worth.

But Tony would never make it to John's. While he was running down the gravel road which ran all the way from their home to the main road, Samuel Peters, clad in a trench coat and hat, was driving along slowly in his black Cadillac, as he looked at street signs. The car turned right at Croton Road. Croton Road had a few houses scattered here and there, but they were sparse. Suddenly, from somewhere in the night, a wild-eyed young boy appeared, running like a madman. Samuel slammed on his brakes. When he got a good look at the boy's face in the headlights, he got excited, "Bingo!" He rolled down the car window, "Hey, kid."

Tony was panting. He leaned over forward with his hands on his knees, trying to catch his breath and said, "Yeah?"

The stranger stuck his hand out the window and handed a picture to Tony. Grinning, the older man asked, "Know where I can find these folks?"

Tony gasped in disbelief when he saw the picture. He could not believe it. In his hand, he held what was a picture of himself along with his sisters. "Who are you?" Tony asked, a bit spooked by this abrupt appearance of the stranger. He was not exactly sure about *any* strangers. This was a long way from the city, and not many strangers made their way out to this gravel road.

"Just get in and I'll tell you, kid."

Tony, exhausted from running so fast and hard, was hesitant, but something told him that he could trust this serendipitous meeting and this stranger. After all, someone had to have given this man the photo he had in his possession, so he climbed into the front seat with Samuel. "But, who sent you?" Tony persisted.

"Trust me on this, kid. It was someone who very definitely is a friend and is on your side."

As the car made its way back down the road from where Tony had just come, if one had been looking, they would have seen on the license plate written in big, bold letters, the state of TENNESSEE.

Once back inside the girls' room, Tony gently shook Rose awake again. When she opened her eyes, Tony, the stranger, Karen and Anna hovered over her. Startled, Rose asked, "What's going on, Tony?"

Moved with compassion at the pitiful sight of the young girl in her bed who was obviously severely beaten, Samuel chocked back his tears. "Come on, sweetheart. You're going home."

Rose was confused at first. "But, where's Daddy?"

The stranger let out a soft, kind and good natured laugh. "Let's just say that he's going to be tied up for a little while, sweetheart." Wrapping her blanket around her, he lifted Rose out of the bed and carried her down the stairs, with the other children following.

The Ancient Paths

While they left out the front door, Jose lay in his bed, bound and gagged with duct tape across his mouth. It would seem that his time of reckoning had come.

"What's your name, mister?" Rose whispered.

"You can call me Sam, sweetie."

"Thank you, Sam. Are you an angel?"

"No, honey. I still have a long way to go before I earn my wings."

"Where are you taking us, Sam?" Rose asked.

"Your first stop, young lady, will be at your grandparents' home."

Sam gently placed Rose in the back seat of the car. Anna and Karen climbed into the back seat with their sister, and Tony took the seat next to Sam in front. In spite of her pain and her battered condition, when the car doors were closed and the car began its slow journey down the long, winding gravel road which lead to the place that had been home for three years now, Rose stared out the window and strained for one last look.

Sam could see her in the rearview mirror. "Sometimes it's best not to look back, sweetheart."

Part 2

CHAPTER 14

Accompanied by Emma and Clarence, now looking worn out and tired, the four children arrived at Wendell Smith's Restaurant where Margie worked as a waitress. Rose was helped along by Anna and Karen. She was still sore from the beating she had taken from her father. As they entered the neighborhood meat and three style restaurant, they could tell for certain that they were back in the south. A Jim Reeves or Hank Williams song was blaring from the jukebox in the corner and the smell of homemade barbeque and cornbread assaulted their senses.

When the four siblings first saw their mother again, it was not exactly the way they had imagined it would be, but she was their mom and they were darn glad to see her, no matter what. They had never thought of her as a waitress. She had always just been mommy or mom before. She was different now, just as they all undeniably knew that they, too, were different. She looked older than they had remembered her, but no less beautiful to them. Karen had been so young when she last saw her mother that she only had vague memories of what her mother was like. But not Rose, she remembered every detail of her beautiful mother's face, the sparkle in her eye and the music of her laughter.

The Ancient Paths

Margie's once curly, flowing natural auburn colored hair was now fire red and styled into a French twist. Her eyebrows were thicker and now dark black from all of the eyeliner pencil she used to mark them up. She was still beautiful in her white waitress pant uniform and white shoes though, and she was their mom! Anna and Karen let go of Rose's arm where they had been holding on to her, and they and Tony took off running as fast as they could through the restaurant, as the heads of customers turned and watched.

Margie knelt down and waited for their embrace. They slammed into her open arms and against her body with such impact that she was thrown backwards and they all fell to the ground laughing, as customers broke into laughter along with them and applauded. "Mommy, Mommy! We love you!" the three children proclaimed in unity.

However, Rose stood back with Emma and Clarence and waited for her mother to come to her. When Margie was able to finally pull herself up from the floor with the help of Tony, Anna and Karen, she dusted herself off, walked over to where Rose stood and knelt down to look her squarely in the face. "What's wrong honey? Aren't you glad to see Mommy too?" Rose threw her arms around her mother's neck and a reservoir of tears was unleashed…tears of joy and tears of sadness. Joy for the mother she had finally been reunited with, and sadness for the lost years of both her and her siblings' childhoods. She was with her mother now, and her mother would make everything

132

right! That was her hope.

"There, there honey. Mommy's here and you're here now. It's going to be okay. Somehow, it will be." Margie stroked Rose's long hair as she tried to soothe her oldest daughter.

Emma finally spoke up, "Margie, we'll talk about it later, but she's been pretty beat up."

Margie cut her hazel green eyes toward her mother. "What do you mean, Mama? What happened to my little girl?" she asked, as she held Rose so tight that Rose winced from the pain.

"We'll talk later, Margie. In the meantime, I think you need to have a talk with all the children and tell them exactly what their living arrangements will be."

"Mama, can you and Clarence leave the children here for a little while so that they can eat a good meal and give me some time to talk with them?"

"Sure, honey. We'll come back in about an hour. Now you children behave and mind your mama. See you in a little bit."

Almost as if an afterthought, Margie asked, "Where's Sam? I need to thank him for his help in getting my babies back."

"He's gone on to his next assignment, honey. Maybe you can thank him later." And with that, Emma and Clarence were out the door.

Margie seated all her children at a round table and took their orders for supper. It seemed that it was barbeque, cornbread and baked beans for everyone. They had had enough of that tasteless northern food for now. After she had placed their plates of steaming hot food in front of them, Margie sat down with her children. "Little sweeties, I can't tell you how much I have missed you all these years…" She immediately started choking up. The reality that she finally had the children back in Tennessee was just now hitting her. Yet, she still had some not so good news for them. "But, I have got to tell you, I don't have my own place right now. Your Aunt Lil and I have a small, upstairs apartment in an old building. We share the bathroom with the people in the other upstairs apartment. I know that you all have been living in a nice home in New York, and I am afraid I can't give that to you right now."

Rose was starting to get scared by what she was hearing. "So, Mommy, do you want us to go back to New York and live with Daddy again?"

"No, Rose. That will never happen. I will never want you to go back and live with your father again. I know what a horrible person he can be. That was why I tried to so hard to get you all back here in Tennessee. However, until whatever time I can have enough money and have my life together enough to have you all with me all the time,

I have arranged for you to live with Grandmommie and Poppy. You can come and visit me and spend the night with me and Aunt Lil, but your home for now will be with your grandparents."

Tony had been listening and soaking it all in. "Sure Mom, whatever you say. We're just glad to be here."

Karen had different thoughts on the subject. She folded her little arms and stuck out her bottom lip. "I don't want to, Mommy. *We* want to live with you!"

Rose was beside herself. "Mommy! We came all the way back here to be with you, and now we can't. Is that what you're saying?" Rose started to cry again.

Anna was too busy eating her food to worry about talking for the moment.

Margie was visibly upset by the reactions of the girls. She did not want to hurt them in any way, but she could see that this was in fact hurting them; that was the last thing she intended to do. "No, that's not what I'm saying, Rose, not at all. I'm just saying that you can spend the night with me, come and visit me and I will come visit you too. But for now, I can't afford to give you all the nice home I know you need and deserve. Please don't cry. I tell you what, Rose, when Mama and Clarence come back for you all this evening, why don't you go ahead and stay here with me and you can spend the night tonight. Tony, you and the other girls can come over this weekend, together or you can come on different days if you like." Everyone agreed that this was an acceptable plan.

So, Rose parted ways with the other three for the night. She remained behind with her mother at the restaurant. They waited for Aunt Lil to pick them up. Since Margie had not ever learned to drive, Lil was the only one who had a license.

Rose was not prepared for what she saw when Aunt Lil arrived. Wow! Aunt Lil was almost a carbon copy of Margie. She was a few inches shorter and a little plumper than Margie, her hair had been colored an even brighter, brassier red than Margie's and her real eyebrows had been completely shaved off and penciled in with a very dark black eyeliner pencil. And her eyes…Rose couldn't quite get over how big, bright and alert Aunt Lil's hazel blue eyes were. Lil, too, was dressed in a white waitress uniform. The second Lil arrived at Wendell Smith's, she grabbed Rose and began gushing over the girl. "Hi, sweetie. You sure are a pretty little thing. I remember when you were just a baby. Once when my ankle was broken, I hopped around on one foot trying to take care of you and change your diapers." Rose was embarrassed by the comment.

"It's funny I don't remember that, Aunt Lil."

Lil was tickled by Rose's naïve comment. "Well, honey, why would you remember that? You were only five or six months old then."

"Oh. Well, Tony said he remembered being born," Rose interjected.

Margie was ready to leave the restaurant and get home. "Come on girls, we're going home and celebrate that my babies are back. Let's do something exciting like...bake a cake or something."

Rose had gotten pretty excited for half a second when she thought they might do something exciting, like maybe go to a movie; but the wind suddenly went out of her sails when she learned that her mom thought of baking a cake as being exciting. "Oh well, it may not be exciting, but at least if it's chocolate, it will make me happy," she mused. Thinking about chocolate led her to remember the beating she had recently endured, all in the name of chocolate. Besides, she had just had the longest ride from New York and she was still bruised and sore, so maybe sitting in a movie wasn't really such a good idea after all.

Their apartment was not far from Margie's work, and when they pulled up in front of the old, two story red brick building they lived in on New York Avenue, Rose immediately started having déjà vu like mad. "Why New York Avenue? Why not...Pennsylvania Avenue, or France Avenue or something else besides stupid *NEW YORK AVENUE*? She had just left New York behind her and she had hoped it was for good; now, here she was at her mother's apartment on NEW YORK AVENUE, in Nashville no less! How do you get New York Avenue in Nashville, Tennessee anyway?" her mind screamed to her.

Margie and Lil could not help but notice how difficult it was for Rose to climb the single flight of stairs that led to their second floor apartment, but they were reluctant to say anything to her about her slow pace. When they finally arrived at the landing at the top of the stairwell, Rose was huffing and puffing. "Whew!" was all she could manage to say. Margie knew that climbing these steps should have been an easy feat for most eleven-year-old girls.

Once inside the apartment, Rose slowly looked around and took in her surroundings. "Wow," she thought to herself." The place was small. There was no denying that, but somehow, it still felt like home to Rose, even though it was not the big home in the rural area where she had been living for the past few years. At least her mom was here now. That one thought seemed to be the answer to all her doubts. The tile on the kitchen floor was the cheap linoleum kind, the kitchen windows were covered by faded yellow lace curtains and the smell of stale coffee seemed to float through the entire apartment. Stale coffee wasn't so bad.

There was one small bedroom which had very little décor, except for the array of make-up and hair products which Rose noticed located on the antiquated dresser with the mirror in the bedroom. This room had the smell of hairspray and makeup which mingled with the stale coffee. And what was that other smell which was layered over all the other scents she was detecting? Oh yeah, that was cigarettes! Oh boy, this was going to be hard, as Rose detested the smell of cigarettes. She needed to find the bathroom, and quick. The stress of recent days, as well as the excitement of returning home to Tennessee seemed to hit her all at once. Or, perhaps it was the combined effect of all the odors in the apartment and her nerves, but suddenly she felt queasy beyond her imagination.

Only the bathroom was outside. She had seen it on the way in. It was, in fact, on the outside of the apartment, and it was indeed shared with the other tenants of the second floor. Well, she would just have to hope that no one was already in there! She was so nauseated, when she walked through the living room on her way out, she didn't notice her mother was on the phone.

As she exited through the kitchen door of the apartment, she turned left, and voila! There was the door to the bathroom. This was different. A community shared bathroom was something she had never experienced before and she was a bit scared who she might run into. She put her hand on the knob, took a deep breath, hesitating before entering. Once she opened the door and stepped in, she let out a gasp. "Oh my gosh, this can't be too sanitary," she said out loud to herself. This room was the piece de resistance. There was a tub to the right of the room, which was a community bathtub, and was corroded, from what she could tell. There was the same cheap linoleum tile in the bathroom as in her mother's kitchen, but never mind that. Her mind quickly moved on to her business at hand. She felt nauseous from the smell of the cigarette smoke, and when she stepped in front of the bathroom mirror and saw her reflection staring back at her, she realized that she was looking a little green around the gills. Turning on the faucet and splashing some cold water over her face helped to quell the nausea a bit.

Was it her imagination, or was she hearing voices outside the bathroom door? She quickly opened the bathroom door and looked around the landing. No one was there. She stepped back into the bathroom and locked the door, only to realize that she was still hearing the voices. Then it hit her; the voices, she realized, were coming from inside her mother's apartment. She had been taught never to eavesdrop on conversations, but that had never stopped her before. She grabbed the single glass cup which sat on the bathroom sink and held it to the wall, and boy, those walls really were thin.

She first heard her Aunt Lil talking. "What did Mama have to say?"

Margie sounded visibly shaken with her voice close to breaking. "She said that son of a gun beat my girl with a razor strap belt! God, Lil. I should have been there for my kids. I can't deal with this! Have you got any valium? That diet pill kicked my butt today and my nerves can't take it right now."

The Ancient Paths

There was no way Rose would have known that during the first year they had all disappeared and their mother did not know where they were, or if they were even alive, she had come close to having a nervous breakdown. And in her desperation, she had reached out for comfort, and had found that comfort in taking drugs. When she felt down, out and destitute, the pills would pick her back up and get her going again. Only, once you were up, you still had to come back down.

In shock, Rose lowered the glass. Had she heard that right? Her mother on diet pills...and valium? She was reeling now. All of a sudden, once again, her world began to spin out of control. Why did it have to be this way?

CHAPTER 15

Even though Rose now understood that while they were away their mother had changed, she loved her more than anyone or anything in the world. It simply did not matter to Rose that her mother was less than perfect. All reasoning went out the window when it came to the issue of loving her mom. After all, hadn't their father been *way* less than perfect? While he may have had the nice home with lots of land, he seemed to have been void of kindness toward his children. Margie may not have had the beautiful home or lots of property, but she had the love for her children, even if she was having some problems at the present, and Rose eagerly looked forward to each visit to her mother's little upstairs apartment. She didn't even mind the smell of cigarettes anymore, as she had grown accustomed to the scent.

Rose didn't know why, but the old, rundown part of town where Margie and Lil lived held a sort of fascination for her. In the beginning, she had been a bit shocked at the conditions in which they lived, but Margie and Lil knew how to hang loose, and Rose had fun with them.

Rose loved her grandmother, and was tremendously grateful to her for taking in her and her siblings, but one thing she had quickly learned about Grandmommie was that she was very old fashioned. Rose was going through a rebellious stage after being freed from the confines for their father's care, and she would be darned if she was going to wear rolled down bobby socks at her age and hemlines down past her knee! In the end, she found it difficult to stay at Grandmommie's home. Simultaneously, she realized that since she was now spending the majority of her time at her mother's apartment, she was seeing less and less of Anna, Karen and Tony. For some reason though, Tony and her sisters didn't seem to be having the difficulty adapting to living with their grandmother that Rose had encountered. Perhaps it was because Clarence had bought a motorcycle for Tony, and Anna and Karen were still young enough that their bodies and their hormones weren't going through the same changes as Rose's, but by the time school started in the fall, Rose had completely moved in with her mother and Lil. The couch was her bed.

One morning, as Rose lay on the couch yawning and stretching while trying to wake up, she saw Lil as she was about to head out the kitchen door for work. Aunt Lil looked over her shoulder at Margie who was sitting at the table sipping coffee, "Jay's coming over tonight."

"Alright, that'll be good."

"Who's Jay?" Rose called out from the next room. She was curious.

"Oh, he's just a friend," Lil smiled with that smirky grin of hers. Rose cocked her eyebrow questioningly at her aunt. She wasn't so sure she believed Lil. She would see for herself if Jay was "just a friend."

"Yeah, right, Aunt Lil! When pigs fly he's your friend!" Giggling like a young schoolgirl, Lil waved goodbye and walked out the door.

"Mom, aren't you going to work today?" Rose queried her mother.

"No honey. I don't feel too good today, so I called in sick. I should be better by tomorrow though." Rose wondered what could be wrong with her mother, but she didn't ask any questions. She didn't want Margie to feel that she was treating her like a child or doubting her in any way.

That afternoon when school let out Rose hurried home to eat something and take a nap. She couldn't wait to see her mom and check on her. While she loved living with her mother and aunt, she had not exactly made a lot of friends at school yet, and adults seemed to be the only people whose company she enjoyed that much at present, especially since she didn't get to see her brother and sisters all the time now. They had always been her best friends before, but now there was a definite distance growing between them. She missed them all, and would see them on occasion when they came to visit, but Rose had not visited them at Grandmommie's house for a while now. She was

144

missing her family. And yet, right now, at this moment in time, she was having an adventure with her mom and Aunt Lil, and she wasn't going to miss out on meeting Lil's "friend" Jay for anything.

Upon entering their small upstairs apartment, Rose wandered through the kitchen, the living room and found her mother in the bedroom, sitting in front of the mirror primping. Instinctively Rose thought, "Mom must be feeling better." She scrutinized her mother's look carefully. Margie had painted her eyebrows a heavy black with lots of eyeliner pencil. Her hair was shoulder length, and whereas it had been up in a French twist yesterday, it was now hanging loosely around her shoulders, with only the upper portion backcombed and put up into a sort of beehive hairdo. Margie sprayed the finishing touch to her hair, and then picked up the perfume bottle and gave herself a squirt.

"Mom," Rose started, and then tried to figure out what to say next. "Um... Mom?"

"What is it sweetie?" Margie asked as she picked up her burning cigarette from the ashtray. She gave it a quick puff and exhaled a long stream of smoke, which Rose watched until it slowly fell apart in the atmosphere.

Rose was always fascinated with her mother and Aunt Lil's grooming rituals. They almost seemed otherworldly to her at times in their precision of their beautification process. Only today, the eyebrows seemed a little too much to Rose. They made her mother look older than she really was.

It hadn't taken Rose long to realize that her mother was a very popular lady. Margie was beautiful, she was sweet, and men and women alike loved her. Wherever they were together in public, Rose was amazed at how people seemed to be drawn to her mother, but she understood it, because she was mesmerized by her mother as well. Rose was so proud of her mother's beauty, that sometimes she almost felt a twinge of jealousy. "But, that's ridiculous," she would think to herself, "how can I be jealous of my own mom?" So, she just accepted that there were times when she both adored her mother and simultaneously, she would feel that nudge, prompting her toward jealousy of her mother's beauty and apparent popularity. Men in particular seemed to be at full attention when Margie was around. Rose would not let those negative thoughts dominate her love for her mother. Besides, maybe she would one day have as many friends who loved her as her mother did.

"Uh," Rose continued, "you look nice, Mom. Are you feeling better now?"

"Yeah. I guess so, sweetie. I thought I would try to make myself feel better by getting cleaned up before Jay gets here tonight."

"Gee, Mom. You look so good, are you sure he's not *your* date?" Rose tried to make light of the situation, only she could not figure it out. Why was her mother getting so cleaned up for her sister's boyfriend this evening?

Margie shot her a fixed, stern look. Rose instinctively knew she had just crossed a line.

"Listen young lady, there is no need for that. I just thought that maybe we could all go out and get a bite when Jay gets here. That's all."

"Me too, Mom?" For some reason, Rose was a bit taken back by her mother's suggestion, but she wasn't sure why. Maybe it was because she had never been invited to an outing of this sort with both male and female adults before.

"Well, of course you too, Rose," Margie chuckled in the good natured manner which Rose had come to love. "We wouldn't want to leave you here alone."

At that very moment, Lil threw open the door to the kitchen and bristled in, throwing down her purse, then fumbling with untying the work apron she still had on. "I have to hurry. I need to shower and Jay will be here in an hour." She threw down the apron, and rushed into the bedroom, looking for some clean clothes.

"Hey, Lil," Margie ventured.

"Yeah. What is it, honey?"

"Think you and Jay will be up for us all going out to get a bite tonight?"

Rose held her breath. She wasn't sure how adults worked this stuff, but she was skeptical that Lil would be amenable to her sister and her sister's daughter tagging along on her date.

"Sure, why not?" Lil flippantly responded. And with that, she was out the door and off to the shower.

Left alone in the room with only her mother again, Rose's only thought was, "Wow, that was kind of...cool."

That evening when the knock on the door came, and Lil, who was now dressed to the hilt with her golden slip on slippers, tight white pedal pushers, floral print blouse and hoop earrings, answered the door, Rose could not have been more taken aback by what walked *through* the door.

Jay was not even young. He was not even handsome. He wasn't even anything at all like what Rose would have imagined Aunt Lil's boyfriend would look like. Into the apartment instead strolled an aging man with a distinct swagger, a wrinkled face, a mouth that was puckered as if he were losing his teeth, wearing a cocked brown suede hat, a smirk as big as the state of Texas, with a burning cigarette hanging out the corner of his mouth.

"Hello, Doll," he drawled in his Southern twang. Rose had always wondered how some people could still talk even with a lit cigarette in their mouth. After daintily removing the burning twig from his mouth, Jay leaned down and smooched Lil on the cheek. "How's my Big Red tonight? I've brought you some little jewels," he snickered.

"Well, alright then, Jay. Honey, this here is my niece, Rose." Lil had promptly tried to change the subject.

He closed one eye as if he was drunk, but Rose did not smell any alcohol. As a matter of fact, he wreaked heavily of aftershave, yet he was obviously intoxicated with something. "Hey, little Princess, nice to meet ya." He extended his hand to her. Rose shyly took his hand. "Guess what I have in my pocket, Rose."

Rose was at a loss for things to guess, so she simply shrugged her shoulders.

"I have a little green man in my pocket," Jay cracked up laughing at himself.

"Oh? Well let's see him then," Rose challenged him.

"You think you're smart, don't ya kid? Well, you can't see the little green man until you have one of my little jewels. Want to see my little jewels?"

"Stop it, Jay!" Lil snapped.

"No, it's okay. Sure, show me your little jewels, Jay." Rose was intrigued. Little green men, little jewels? "Whatever it is, just lay it on me," she thought.

Margie groaned audibly, "Oh my God," while wringing her hands.

Against the protests of both Margie and Lil, Jay reached in his pocket and extracted a handful of various colored pills. "We have Yellow Jackets, Black Jackets and Valiums."

Slowly and deliberately, with a firm grip, Lil grasped his wrist with one hand, and with the other, wrapped her fingers around his hand and balled it into a fist, then guided his hand back into his pocket. She knew he was already way too high. "Oh, don't pay attention to him, sweetie. Jay, honey, you know better than to carry that kind of stuff around with you. Where did you get that stuff anyway?" Instantly, she realized she had said too much. When Jay opened his mouth to answer, Lil quickly removed her hand from his wrist and clamped it over his mouth. "Quit playing tricks on Rose, you silly boy." She tried to laugh off the incident, but the cat was already out of the bag, so to speak. Or to be more precise, the pills were already out of the pocket.

"Just remember this," Rose thought to herself, "no matter how bad this looks, at least you're not in New York now."

CHAPTER 16

Rose had long been aware that neither of her parents were perfect, especially her father. After her introduction to Jay, there was little room for doubt in her mind that her mother and Lil were pill poppers too. Perhaps there had been a small measure of validity in some of her father's statements about her mother; and yet, none of the cruel, hateful, demeaning things he had ever spoken about her mom could begin to compare to the truths she knew only too well about her dad.

Rose knew very well that her mother had been missing work a lot lately, and she had been withdrawn, which was unusual for someone with a bright and cheerful personality like her mom. However, nothing could have prepared Rose for what she found when she arrived home from school that day. The moment she stepped into the kitchen, the atmosphere had a different quality to it. Even though the usual scent of fresh brewed coffee filled the thick, hot air, there was a quiet and stillness which lingered in the home this day. Then she heard it, the muffled sounds of something that sounded like a tap, tap, tapping in the back bedroom, in her mother's room. It was a dull pounding noise. She was frightened and unsure whether to proceed forward or not. "But what if something has happened to her? What if someone is hurting her?"

She looked around for something, anything she could grab onto, and eyeballing the iron skillet on the stove, she grabbed it. It was heavier than she had realized, so she had to use both hands to lift it up over her right shoulder. With her pulse beating rapidly and her breathing becoming so labored, she was hearing her own breath now. Trying to stay calm and focused by taking a deep breath, she sucked in all her air and moved on.

Expecting at any moment to see someone jumping from behind the wall with a sledge hammer, a knife or a gun, Rose was shocked beyond her wildest imagination when instead, she came upon what she now saw was the frail looking figure of her mother. Kneeling on the floor with a hammer and a screwdriver, banging on the metallic vent of the window air conditioner, was Margie. She was dressed in too pretty a green full skirt to be kneeling on the floor. On the floor beside her was her little glass ashtray with its lit cigarette, as usual.

"Mom, what's wrong with the air conditioner?"

Startled, Margie gasped, "Ah!" and sprang up off the dirty wood floor, almost falling backward as she stood. She was shaking like a leaf, with the hammer still in her hand. "Nothing, nothing at all!"

Rose muttered slowly, "So, Mom, why are you trying to fix it then?"

Margie's eyes darted around the room and beyond. Glaring at her daughter with a deer in headlights expression, she whispered, "Rose, come here," motioning with her free hand.

Her mom was scaring her just a little bit. "Mom, I'm *already* here. What's wrong?"

"Shh!" Margie cautioned.

"What is it?" Rose whispered in response.

"They'll hear you," Margie whispered back.

"Who will hear me, Mom?" asked Rose.

"I got it figured out, honey. Jay and Lil...they have been listening to me. I'm looking for the wire they used. I think it's in the air conditioner."

Rose's facial expression reflected her surprise. She wasn't sure what was true at that moment—if it were true that Jay and Lil had tried to listen in on her mom for some reason. If that were the case, then they would also have had to listen in on Lil as well, meaning that Lil was listening in on herself. Yet somehow, Rose was not beyond believing it was possible. As far as that went, they would also have to be listening in on Rose. She was looking at the air conditioner, and as far as she knew, which really wasn't saying much, there did not seem to be anything which looked so unusual about the way it was wired, but what did she know? So, what was the truth?

"Mommy," Rose began cautiously, "are you okay? Did you...take something today?"

Margie looked nervously around the room. "Nothing out of the ordinary, Rose. Just a Yellow Jacket. Well, maybe it was two. I don't remember, but anyway, that's okay. I have a valium I can take when I'm ready."

Rose was becoming more and more fearful for her mother's well-being by the second. "Mom, now might be a good time to take that valium."

"This might not be New York...but it was in fact, New York Avenue, wasn't it" Rose pondered, as she absentmindedly reached for her mother's cigarettes on the bed, picked up the BIC lighter and lit one up. She took a long, deep drag and held her breath, mulling over the situation. "Yes," she concluded, her mother probably needed some help.

Breathing heavily and glaring at Rose in disbelief, Margie asked, "So, Missy, when did *you* start smoking?" Margie's senses were intensified ten-fold at the moment, so she was still aware enough to realize her twelve-year-old daughter had just lit a cigarette.

"Oh! What? Was I smoking?" Rose gagged as she realized that she was holding the cigarette, then nervously snuffed it out in her mother's ashtray.

CHAPTER 17

It had been an inevitability that Rose would sooner or later end up back at Grandmommie's house. With every fiber of her being, she knew it the day she came home and her mother was looking for wires which she believed had been used to bug their apartment. Margie though, had been quite reluctant to call her mother and ask for permission to come back home at her age and start over. Lil, however, was wild and determined she would not go back home to her mother's, so she just decided she would do the only logical thing--shack up with Jay.

The bus ride across town only took a little while, and then Margie and Rose had to walk from the main road, down the long side street, to the right a block, and then to the left down the gravel road to the dead end. The day that Margie and Rose arrived at Grandmommie's, the reunion between Rose, Tony, Anna and Karen was joyous, and simultaneously, a little subdued. Was it Rose's imagination that Anna and Karen now seemed so much more than just little girls? And that Tony was growing into such a mature teenage boy? Rose found herself wondering, "Where have I been? I can't believe how much everyone has changed, just since we came back to Tennessee." Rose had to fight back the tears, as she realized just how much she had missed seeing her siblings.

Anna and Karen were happy to see her too, but Tony seemed a little more aloof. "Hey, Sis. Good to see you." He gave her a quick slap on the back.

Margie, too, was emotional, as she had not seen her three other children nearly as much as she would have liked to. She was acutely aware of the fact that she was missing out on the lives of her three other children by the day. "Come here, sweeties. Give Mommy a hug." Anna, Karen and Tony fell into her arms and wrapped their arms around her. "I'm sorry I haven't seen you all more. Mommy hasn't been feeling well."

Tony gave his mom a peck on the cheek, and without so much as another word, he was out the door to go for a ride on his motorcycle. Rose knew her brother well, and she could see that he was wrestling with his own bundled up emotions over the twists and turns their lives had taken since returning to the south. It was not exactly like either of them had imagined it would be, she knew. Coming back to Tennessee was supposed to have made them all closer, happier and freer! So, what had gone so terribly wrong?

Anna and Karen had an announcement to make to Rose. "Hey, guess what, Sissy?"

"What?"

"We found a really fun place to go for walks. Want to see?" Rose did not feel like going for a hike, especially after the long walk from the main road, and it was really hot now. The south always had those blistery hot and exhausting, humid days, but looking at her sisters' eager little faces, she simply could not bring herself to disappoint them.

"Sure. Why not? Is that okay with you, Mom?"

Margie was relieved. Now maybe she could have a moment alone with *her* mother who had been standing to the side of the room, quietly taking in everyone's reactions to the situation. "Sure honey, you go ahead. Me and Grandmommie have some things to discuss anyway." When she finally dared to steal a glance at Emma's face, she recoiled at the piercing, stark glare of her own mother.

With Anna or Karen on either side of her, Rose headed out the door to see her sisters' new discovery. "Where are we going?" she wanted to know.

Anna was reassuring. "It's okay, sis. Just hold our hands and we'll lead you, but you can still keep your eyes open so you don't fall."

"Oh, so I don't have to walk with my eyes closed and fall down?
159

How sweet of you, Anna."

Anna and Karen each slipped a hand through Rose's, then Anna enthusiastically shouted, "Let's run!" And with that, the two younger sisters jerked Rose out of her fog, and even though their legs were a bit shorter than Rose's, she had to focus in order to keep up with them. They must have been spending a lot of time outdoors playing, she thought. It soon became obvious that where they were taking her was to the dried out creek bed where there were plenty of small rocks in place of the water which had been there before the weather had gotten so hot and dry. Drought every few years in the region was not altogether uncommon.

"I don't know if I want to go down to the creek," she began. She had not once been to the creek since they had returned to Nashville. While she had fond memories of the creek in Hickman County where Grandmommie had raised her mother, her aunts and her uncles, Rose never knew why she hadn't wanted to visit the creek at Grandmommie's new place. She had never even seen the creek there. She remembered the fun trips to the old holler in the summers before Margie and Jose had divorced. Her most recent times when she had played in water had been at the creek in New York, when she had wished they had a raft which would carry them away from their father and the hell they had lived in there. She had to shrug off those thoughts and feelings now.

The Ancient Paths

By the time Rose had stopped daydreaming, she was already standing in front of the dry creek, and her sisters were crossing over the dry creek bed and shouting and pointing, "Come on, Rose! Look!" As she followed the direction of her sisters' pointing fingers, she now saw for the first time also, a huge wooded area. The younger girls were running and laughing.

Suddenly, Rose felt a surge of excitement and energy as she bolted into a full gait after her sisters. "You little rascals, I'll catch you." Anna and Karen squealed with delight and ran with all their might as their big sister pursued them in a game of chase. Rose now realized just exactly how much she had missed her siblings. It seemed to her they hadn't played together like this in a very long time.

CHAPTER 18

"What do you mean, I can't take my own daughter to the square? That's ridiculous, Mother, and you know it!" Margie was incensed and hurt that her mother could say such a thing to her. "Rose asks me if we can walk up to Madison Square, a little over half a mile from here, and you tell me I can't take her. Well, for your information, Mother, she is my daughter!"

"You listen to me, girlie," Emma snapped, "you're not right. You're on those pills again, and I don't know if you can be trusted to take her anywhere."

Margie's anger was now at the boiling point, and Rose was standing in the far corner of the room taking it all in. "I haven't taken a pill since I got here yesterday. I came here in the hopes of starting over, but you're making it rather difficult, Mother!" She marched across the room to where Rose stood and took her daughter by the hand. "Come on Rose, we're going." Before they could get out the door, Emma had grabbed Margie by the left arm, whirled her around and began slapping her repeatedly in the face. Emma then threw Margie up against the wall and started pounding her head against the wall. Margie tried to restrain her mother by grabbing her wrists, but Emma

162

wrenched her hands free and resumed pounding her daughter's head against the wall.

Rose watched the scene unfold in horror. What in the heck was going on here? Where was everybody when she needed them? Clarence was at work, Tony was out riding his motorcycle that Clarence had bought him and the girls were off somewhere playing. For a split second she felt shock was going to take over, but complete numbness was what she wanted to feel at that moment. Hadn't they moved here to get away from violence and abuse? She sobbed hysterically as she screamed, "Stop it! Stop it!" as she pulled her mother toward the door and away from her grandmother. Rose had not known she possessed such strength in her little body. Her grandmother was a physically strong woman, but she knew that somehow she had to get her mother out of there, and she yanked Margie free from Emma's grip.

As soon as Rose had wrenched Margie's arm from Emma's grip, Emma turned and slapped Rose and sent her stumbling into the wall. Rose never knew what strength menopause could give a woman! She lunged past her grandmother and grabbed Margie's arm again and this time pulled her out the door as Emma's fists landed repeatedly on Margie.

Emma was still yelling as they made their way out of the front yard, "You can't take her! I'll call Children's Services on you!"

"Go ahead, Mama. You call 'em, but I'll never come back home to you again," Margie sobbed. She had not once raised her hand to strike her mother back. She could have, but she would never hit her mother. "I can't believe Mama would do that," she cried. "I know I have disappointed her a lot, but I really just wanted to go to the shopping center with you for a while today."

"I know, Mommy. I can't believe she did that either. What's wrong with her?"

"I guess she thinks I'm crazy and that I'm not responsible enough to take care of my own child, even long enough to walk to the store. I guess we have to find a place to stay again, Rose, unless you want to stay here at Mama's."

Rose couldn't believe what was happening. After all, it was literally only yesterday that she and her mother had finally come home to Emma's to live for a while, and now they were already having to leave. Rose was mentally and emotionally exhausted. "Mommy, I can't stay with Grandmommie. I can't believe she did that stuff. I feel bad about Anna and Karen though. They're going to wonder what happened to us. They're going to think that we don't want them and that we're just always going to leave them." The poor girl was understandably distraught at this point about having to once again leave her little sisters that she had only months ago been in New York acting as surrogate mother to.

164

"We'll talk to them as soon as we can, honey, but for now I have to think of a place for us to stay."

"What about with Aunt Lil?"

"That would be a good idea, except that she's living with John, honey. Remember? So that's out of the question. I guess I'll call the Salvation Army."

"What? What's the Salvation Army, Mommy?"

"The Salvation Army is a place that is funded by donations, and it helps people in times of trouble. I've heard that sometimes they will give you a place to stay."

"Well, alright then. Please call them, Mommy." Together, the twosome could make decisions. Rose suddenly felt that she, too, had to be grownup and strong for her mother, just as Margie knew she needed to be big and strong for Rose, even though there were times when she felt as though she herself were not much more than a child. After all, she had been a mere child herself when she had married that monster Jose so long ago now. She was so young when she had started giving birth to her own children.

Fortunately, Margie already had her purse dangling from her arm when Rose had pulled her out the door. She did have at least a little money with her. After stopping at a phone booth to call and inquire of the Salvation Army, Margie informed Rose, "We can stay there for a week. Let's go. We have a bus to catch."

At dusk, when the haggard looking pair came dragging in at the Salvation Army, they were greeted by a shift supervisor. "So glad we were able to provide you with some assistance, Margie. Yeah, I knew it was you because you and your daughter are the only females staying here tonight. You will find that the accommodations are clean and you will receive three meals a day."

"Thank you, but what about…"

As if reading her mind, the supervisor interrupted her, "Don't worry. We're going to help you. We have made arrangements for you to talk with a social worker to see if you can get the help you need, and to see if we can find a good place for Rose to stay until you are able to take care of her."

Rose was reeling, and all the while, thoughts raced through her mind, "Did he say "social worker…find a good place for me to stay?" Surely she was not getting on that merry-go-round again. What did it mean to have a social worker this time? They had one before that took them away from their mother. Would they just…take her away from her mother again? "Please, God, don't let that happen," she prayed. In her mind, she reasoned with the invisible God she had always heard so much about from her grandmother; the one she felt moved to dance and sing to when she was younger. "Wasn't that why we came back to Tennessee anyway, to have a good place to stay and to have a normal life again?" But in her heart, Rose knew that her life was still anything but normal. Please don't let this be a trick, dear Lord." She gritted her teeth and listened to the plan.

CHAPTER 19

And so it was. Rose spent ten months in a children's home while Margie went to the psychiatric unit in the hospital to dry out and try to reclaim her life. Even though every day that went by, Rose could think of nothing else except when she would be out in the world again, she had grown up considerably as a result of her constant exposure to a houseful of other teens. The friendships she had made during her stay at the home had been sweet, real, and at times volatile, but she had come to love her newfound friends.

The day that Rose was released from the children's home, there was much crying and hugging as she bade farewell to the girls who had been her confidants and family for the past ten months. It was difficult to say if it was harder on Rose, or on the other girls, to say goodbye. Rose knew for sure that her heart was breaking yet again.

Rose and her mom stepped outdoors into the warm summer air and for a split-second Rose could only feel disbelief. She had made it. She had waited out her time in the home and now…she was free! "Oh my gosh," she thought, "I'm out!" She wept as she left her home of the last ten months. Just beyond the sidewalk, her mother's new husband, Nick waited in the car for them. Nick was a big, baldheaded Greek man with black framed glasses. When Rose had first met Nick, he didn't look like the type of man Rose would have guessed her mom to marry, but Rose had quickly warmed up to him over the last few months, as she liked his personality and her mom really liked him. He had made her mom smile again.

Rose climbed into the back seat of the long olive green Oldsmobile and quickly looked out the window and waved good bye to her friends as they stood in the doorway waving back. It seemed so long ago now that she had entered the children's home, tired and worn out, anxious and upset that she still would not be with her mother for a while longer, and yet reluctant to return to the care of her grandmother. Rose loved her grandmother and she knew she had meant well, but after seeing how Emma had so quickly turned on both Margie and herself that day, Rose could not stop comparing the violence she had experienced at the hand of her father with the violence she had seen Emma unleash on them that day. So, no, she had not been able to make herself go back there. Now she was on her way to her new home with her mom and her new stepdad.

"Where are we going, Mommy?" Rose asked. While Rose was now a young teenager, she had not managed to make herself stop calling Margie "Mommy." She had tried to outgrow it, but she just hadn't been able to make herself refer to Margie as "Mama" yet.

"Well, we wanted a place big enough that Tony and the girls could live with us, so Nick found a nice home on Murphy Road not far from here, and you'll still go to the same school." Rose clapped her hands in excitement, just like a small child would. She had dreaded the possibility that she may have to change schools again.

The house was only moments away from the children's home, so the area was not unfamiliar to Rose. It was in a nice, quiet neighborhood, and when they pulled into the driveway, Rose was surprised. There seemed to be a stillness about the place. The house looked like something out of a fairytale, she thought. There was a big shade tree and a birdbath in the front yard. The driveway led up to the side porch, which actually served as the main entrance to the house. On the porch was a wooden swing hanging by chains. The dark, red brick with the window panes trimmed in white gave the house a very cottage like appearance. The home was two stories high and had a window on the second floor which looked out over the main street. This looked like a place where they would have some peace.

Rose felt oddly out of her element. Almost constantly, for the past ten months, she had been with a large group of young women. They had had a house mother who ruled the roost and whom everyone went to with their questions. Right now she was happy and sad at the same time, full of so many emotions that she couldn't count them. As she meandered first through the living room, dining room and kitchen, she was lost in thought. So when she opened her bedroom door to check it out, she was totally caught off guard when her siblings jumped out and screamed, "Surprise!" she lost it. Tony, Anna and Karen hovered around her, hugging her, smiling, laughing and then crying. They all cried. It had been a long time coming.

In spite of her joy at being reunited with her family, she somehow felt that something was different...maybe it was her that had changed. She didn't know and couldn't quite put her finger on it, but it didn't really seem to matter- she had her sisters and her big brother back. Tony had always been close to Rose's heart. She knew he had suffered horribly under the dictatorial parenting of their dad; they all had, but for Tony, it had been much worse. Tony was a good kid and had never given anyone a moment of trouble, but he had been treated so poorly when they were with their dad that it would have driven some young boys to total despair and hopelessness. Rose wondered if any of them would ever truly be happy, but for this moment, she was very happy.

Rose's life was soon to become a revolving door of people in and out of her life; some would remain there for a long time, some would come and go quickly, and there would be those who would stick around longer than she cared for.

CHAPTER 20

Sometimes time itself has a way of bringing about healing…or not. Sometimes we just try to forget the past. And sometimes, we simply bury the past, until whatever time it chooses to rear its ugly head again. That's what Rose, Tony, Anna and Karen did. They had not exactly healed, and they knew they would most likely never forget what they had been through with their father, but they put on brave faces and tried, each in their own way, to forget.

Rose had become a popular young lady at school, especially with the boys, who all seemed to adore her—one in particular, Greg.

Rose posed for a picture with a group of other high school kids. The light flashed and the photographer shouted, "Okay, that's it for the French Club! You're free to go! Next, Wrestling Club, please!" When the French Club group dispersed, a handsome teenage boy with dark hair and deep brown eyes was standing there to meet Rose.

"Hi, Greg!" Rose gushed and blushed. She was positively upbeat and buoyant about her boyfriend. "I'll wait here while you have your picture made," she said. She loved the fact that Greg was so handsome and manly.

The Ancient Paths

As soon as the wrestling team had their photo made, Greg and Rose headed for class together. "Boy, we have to do that poetry thing today, huh?" she asked Greg.

"Yep. Did you get something written, Rose? I did, but barely."

"Well, you'll see. I'm kind of nervous about it though."

The class bell rang and Mrs. Silva called the class to order. "We will call everyone up alphabetically to do their readings today. So, we will start with A's and work our way through the alphabet. If your last name begins with A, you're up!"

It didn't take long to reach names beginning with D, and Rose was up for her turn. The teacher went by De instead of Rivera for Rose's last name. She was very self-conscious about the fact that her name was so different from everyone else's at school. Nobody seemed to know why she had to have "De La" in front of Rivera. She really didn't know either, but that was the name she was born with. No one else at school except her and Tony had three parts to their last name. It didn't seem to actually bother anyone but her. Rose inhaled deeply as she stood up when her name was called. She walked quickly to the podium in front of the class.

Once she was standing there staring out at the sea of faces in the classroom, she had a sudden attack of nerves and she stalled for a brief moment, hesitating, clearing her throat, palms sweating, then she began:

"So there I lay, with nothing to say.

This was my sanity flight,

Back from the long corridors of night.

How I had gotten there was unknown to me.

I suppose it shall remain a mystery.

My virtue had actually been my vice.

Sometimes we do make the same mistake twice.

Now here we stand at the fork in the road

That we all come to, sometime, I am told.

Countless others before me have traveled the path.

I wonder if they thought they would be the last.

But these are only words to express my feelings as they grow

So come on Lord

Let's get on with the show."

Rose stood stiff as a board, holding her breath and glancing around at her classmates, afraid of their response. There was dead silence for a brief moment, so she started toward her seat when all of a sudden applause broke out from every direction in the room. Even Ms. Silva clapped loudly, and Greg was whistling and shouting, "That's my girl!"

Mrs. Silva did not tell her the poem was great or wonderful. Instead, she gave Rose the best compliment anyone could have given her, "Very reminiscent of your brother's poetry, actually, Rose." Rose frequently read her brother's writings and knew that he had a gift, and that she would never attain the level of vocabulary Tony possessed, but she had learned from him indeed.

Tony, himself, was quite popular with the young ladies at school, and he had attained a certain…notoriety, if you will, as one of the first hippies at school. It was the 1970's after all, and life was changing at break-neck speed, not just for Rose and her family, but for many young people. Heck, shortly after they had come back to Nashville, the Woodstock Festival had taken place at Yasgur's Farm about a hundred and fifty miles from their old home in New York.

Cohn High had been known as a redneck school for many years, but now the hippies were coming, ready or not. While Rose was the straight-laced girl next door with the monogrammed shirts and sweaters, Tony had found other outlets for his creative mind. He was intelligent and deep. Rose knew her brother was a thinker; she was the talker. His was a different group of friends altogether, and most of his friends actually went to a school that he considered to be much more hip than the old Cohn High where he was forced to attend with Rose. Rose had to hand it to her brother, he seemed to always know about things way before she ever dreamed they existed. Tony was viewed by many as somewhat of a guru, and Rose knew it. He was one of those that always seemed to be ahead of his time, or at least ahead of most other kids his age.

After class, Greg waited with Rose at her locker while she grabbed their books for the next class. A boy and girl in patched blue jeans and long hair meandered past Rose and Greg giving Rose the thumbs up sign. The boy said very admirably, "Hey. Cool poem, Rose, especially for a brainiac."

Greg couldn't resist and quipped, "Joel, are you insulting my girlfriend, calling her a brainiac, man?" The boy quickly hustled past them and Greg laughed. "I love that guy! I'd like to get him out on the wrestling mat sometime and see if I can toughen him up a little bit!" Rose slapped Greg on the head. He was such a jock.

***

Rose still had a difficult time grasping just how drastically her life had changed. She, Anna, Karen and Tony were no longer treated as prisoners who were there to be subjected to the whims of a madman. They were free now! While she mostly saw the girls from the children's home only in the hallways during school hours now, she still had the comfort of knowing that some of them were there. In increments, that part of her life had begun to fade from memory though.

Rose had begun to experience some sense of normalcy in her life, at least she felt like she was. However, she also knew in her heart of hearts that she had somehow drifted from her siblings, at least from Anna and Karen. Rose felt…well, she felt kind of grown up now, and Anna and Karen still seemed quite young to her. Rose loved them dearly, but was keenly aware that due to coming into her own as a teenager, she was seeing them less and less now, and possibly seeing them through a different lens than she had before. She had waited so long to be reunited with her family, and now she was not spending the kind of time with them that she had hoped to.

***

Rose's best friend was Laurie, a pretty blond with big brown eyes. Laurie was one of the new friends Rose had made since coming to Cohn High School. Laurie was so sweet, but it was possible that Anna and Karen may have been just a tad bit jealous of Laurie. After all, she was the one spending time with their big sis now and they weren't so much. As Anna and Karen sat watching television together on the big velvet orange couch that their stepdad had stolen from the warehouse where he was a night guard (turned out that Nick was a kleptomaniac as a result of the steel plate implanted in his head), they were interrupted by a knock at the front door. Anna reluctantly stood and headed toward the door, but before she could reach it, the front door swung open and Laurie barged in. "Hi, is Rose here? Thanks, I know where to find her!"

The Ancient Paths

Pointing in the direction of Rose's room, Laurie bristled past Anna and threw open the door to Rose's bedroom while Anna was left standing with her mouth wide open, gaping after Laurie. Anna quickly regained her composure, "You know, sometimes I like that girl in spite of myself!"

Rose was surprised and unprepared. Even though she was dressed in her hip-hugger bell-bottoms and a tank top, she still had her hair in her jumbo sized curlers. But, before Rose could object, Laurie took command of the situation. "That looks great! Ready to go?"

"No, I'm not ready to go, Laurie! Look at me. I need to do my nails. You want to do yours too? By the way, how are we getting to the dance tonight?"

"Well, I say yes, let's do our nails, and I thought maybe your stepdad could drive us to the dance." Rose couldn't help but grin. She loved Laurie. She was so unpredictable but so much fun. She had been a bright spot for Rose after leaving the children's home.

The girls sat happily on the floor listening to the radio and polishing their nails when the door opened quietly and Margie stuck her head in. "Rose, you have a phone call, sweetie. It's from New York."

CHAPTER 21

Jose lay in the hospital bed with IVs and tubes running in every direction from his body. Rose sat silently, watching her father. She had honestly not ever considered the possibility that they would actually see one another again. She also never thought about her father dying as being a reality either. While she was a child in New York, she had daydreamed that she would one day kill him if she had had to stay in New York, but she had never considered that her father might just get sick and die young. Now, here it was in front of her. Her father was weak and frail, no longer the energized demon she had remembered. After a while, Jose managed to open his eyes. "How long have you been sitting there, Rose?"

"Um…about an hour." Her voice was low and faint at first. She was not sure what to feel. Should she be afraid? Should she hate him? What??

"Thank you for coming, Rose," Jose gasped.

"Hmm. Well, I suppose it's the least I could do, especially considering that the last time I saw you, you tried to beat me to death!" She may have been a little bit older now, but try as she may have, her

179

bitterness over the past was not dead yet.

Jose turned his head away. "Please don't," he whispered.

However, Rose's anger was unstoppable now that it had been unleashed. It was like a stampede of wild horses coming upon her soul. "I thought it would only be appropriate if I came to see you on your deathbed...***Daddy***."

Tears streamed down her father's face. "I know. I know that I deserve that. I did spank you guys too hard."

Rose jumped up out of her seat. She was incensed at her father's watered down version of what he had done to them. "Too hard? You *spanked* us TOO HARD! Is that all you have to say?" She was between crying and practically shouting now, and the sound of her own voice brought her around to the realization that she needed to get a grip and lower her voice just a bit.

"I told you, Rose. I *know* I deserve your anger, as well as that of your brother and sisters, but please try to control your anger, at least long enough for me to give you something. It's something that I wanted you to have before I go. It was bought for you a long time ago."

"Why would you want to give me anything? Why not Tony or one of the other girls? Why me, Dad? And do they know for sure you're really dying?"

"Because you were different from the others, Rose. They would not know what to do with this." And with that, he reached for the drawer beside his bed.

***

In between classes, Greg and Rose were once again at Rose's locker gathering up books for the next class. Greg walked Rose to her next class and kissed her at the door, the kind of things that young people in love normally did. She was about to walk inside the classroom when he grabbed her arm, pulling her back and turning her around to face him. "I have to talk to you, after school today. Meet me at Kuhn's soda fountain at 3:30, please." She nodded. He knew she would meet him anywhere he asked if she possibly could.

That afternoon, immediately after school let out, Rose walked across Charlotte Pike to meet Greg at Kuhn's. In those days, the soda fountain at Kuhn's Discount Store was one of the many meet up places for kids after school. Rose sipped on a float while she waited for Greg and glanced at the clock every few seconds. Greg was late and it was not like him. The waitress checked to see if Rose needed anything else. Rose shook her head no as she continued glancing at the clock on the wall and began wringing her hands. Where was he?

The Ancient Paths

At exactly three forty-five p.m., Greg threw himself into the seat opposite Rose. He gave her his best pouty facial expression, "I'm sorry honey. Forgive me?"

She couldn't not forgive the boy if she tried. He was simply too darn charming, and she loved having a Southern boy for her boyfriend. He was so different from all the boys she had known in the north—his accent, his hair, all of the little things that were so important. And he was such a gentleman, sometimes that is. She nodded and flashed her most convincing smile. "So, what is it you wanted to talk about, Greg? What's going on? Look at me, please." She was worried because she could tell he was having a hard time looking her in the eyes, plus the fact that he was late. What was going on with him? Had he met someone else? She could feel her pulse racing.

Greg looked away, hesitating, and then slowly, he finally looked up with tears in his eyes. "My dad got transferred on his job. We're moving, Rose, to Michigan."

"What?!" If someone had sucker punched her, she could not have been more breathless. She simply could not believe what she was hearing. She buried her face in her hand and whispered, "You can't. You're the one good thing in my whole life, Greg. You can't just leave me like this."

Greg moved over to sit beside Rose in her seat and put his arms around her. She began to cry softly because she felt her heart was breaking all over again. How many times in one lifetime can a person's heart break? Greg could no longer hold back his tears either.

"I love you, Greg. I never told you because it's so hard for me, but I do love you."

"I love you too, Rose. You've always been the only one for me ever since the day I first saw you, when you first came to school here. I'll come back one day. I promise, and we'll get married." He stroked her hair to comfort her, but Rose could only wonder if their dreams would ever really come true.

The following afternoon, Tony lay on his bed listening to music with his eyes closed. Even though he was immersed in the sounds coming from his turntable, he heard the squeaking of the door at the bottom of the steps which led up to his room. Suddenly, the door slammed shut and there were footsteps pounding on his stairwell from which Rose emerged a moment later. "Tony, man, am I ever glad to see you." Tony jumped up and greeted Rose with a good ole slap on the back. He could always tell when Rose was upset, and she was obviously upset now.

"Long time no see, Sis. What's up and what can I do for you?"

Rose could barely find her voice. "Greg's family is moving away.

His dad got transferred."

"Oh bummer, for sure." The wheels were already turning rapidly in Tony's mind. He could feel his sister's grief. They were not twins, but they had always been close. They had been the two oldest who had tried together to look out for the two younger girls while they had been in New York. Tony, being the older brother, had tried to look out for them all. "Hey, I got something that will cheer you up."

"Yeah? Like what?" she asked, pouting and sticking out her lower lip, which her big brother always hated to see. The lower lip jutting out always meant that his sister was on the verge of being inconsolable.

"Come on. Let's go for a walk, Sis."

***

Tony and Rose approached the entrance to Centennial Park. Young men with long hair, bandanas and beads around their necks either lay on the grass or walked hand in hand with beautiful young women who were clad in bell-bottoms or long, flowing dresses with floral designs and flowers in their hair. Some of the couples danced barefoot in the grass without any music. Rose was thinking to herself, "Wonder when all of this happened. This must be where Tony has been hanging out. Man," she uttered softly. She had heard about all of the young people who now congregated at Centennial Park in Nashville, but she had never been there. This was like a whole new world to Rose.

Rose and Tony slowly made their way through the groups of young people taking their leisure in the sun. In the distance, Rose spotted a teenage boy with shoulder length blondish hair who was walking alone. He meandered along slowly and a short distance behind him, an older man appeared to be following him. Tony noticed this too. The older guy was not being very discreet about the fact that he was following the younger man. Tony grinned at his sister. "Watch this," and with a flick of his wrist, Tony sent his Frisbee sailing across the wide open space in the direction of the two men. The distance he threw it was impressive.

Tony and Rose walked in the direction of the Frisbee, watching as the older man turned to his right and left the scene. As the younger man approached, Tony waved at him. Now Rose was just a bit confused. Rose glared at her brother and asked "You know him?"

Tony ignored her question. "Hey Scott, how'd you like that fancy wrist work?"

Scott was very laid back and smooth. "Yeah, that was groovy."

"There was some old pervert following you, man, but I scared him off with the mighty Frisbee." The boys had a good laugh about Scott being rescued by the Frisbee.

Rose was curious now and could no longer hold her peace. "Okay, Tony, introduce me."

Tony, as always, was the more sophisticated, articulate older brother. "Oh, allow me. Scott, this is my sister, Rose." Rose and Scott nodded to one another and shook hands. Rose couldn't help but notice how blue his eyes were, and how rosy his cheeks were. She wondered if he was Irish.

Tony cleared his throat and the attention of the other two was immediately focused on him again. "Oh, by the way," Tony said, mischievously, as he reached into his pocket and extracted two joints to present to Rose and Scott, "I found these today."

Rose's adrenaline level went through the roof at the sight of marijuana. "Huh? That's how you want me to relax? I don't know, Tony! I don't think so." He could detect the fear in her voice.

"Just think about it for a minute, Rose. It will relax you, and you know you need to relax right now."

She gave it some thought. "Are you sure two will be enough? There's three of us." she asked.

The Ancient Paths

Tony winked at Scott. "Her first time. Follow me, you guys."

The threesome made their way to the miniature band shell which was carved out of stone.

There, they took refuge from the sun by sitting underneath the figure. They carefully took their seats in a small circle. Without saying a word, Tony extended the joint and offered it to Rose, and she in turn, without saying a word, accepted it. Tony struck the match and lit it for her. Try as she may to be cool and nonchalant, after inhaling, Rose gagged and choked, trying desperately to catch her breath. This stuff gagged her worse than the cigarettes she had recently started smoking.

Tony reached for the stick of marijuana and took it from her. Holding up his index finger, he got her attention so that he could demonstrate how it was done. He inhaled slowly and held his breath for a few seconds before slowly exhaling. He then passed the joint to Scott who repeated Tony's actions before passing the joint to Rose.

Rose cautiously accepted the burning stick of weed and smoked it without choking this time. A subtle smile slowly found its way to her face. She took a few more quick short hits on the marijuana cigarette before she lay back on the ground and gazed up into the heavens. She didn't know why she couldn't stop laughing or get the smile off her face. That's just the way it was. She didn't care that Tony and Scott were there. Nothing seemed to matter. The clouds came closer to her and began to spin, when suddenly Tony's voice interrupted her flow. "Okay, Rose, are you ready to go?"

"No, Tony," she protested, shaking her head and laughing.

"Man, she is ripped. That stuff was some of that one toke trip weed from Thailand. That was a joke that she thought we each needed our own. Can you give me a hand, Scott?" The two boys helped Rose to her feet as she slumped, limp as a dish rag in their arms. Tony pat Rose's cheeks a few times trying to get her to snap out of it. "Come on, Rose. We need to get home." She smiled at him, patting him on his face and giggling. Tony was panicking now. "My mom will beat my butt if Rose doesn't pull it together."

Later that evening, Rose lay in her bed, still sufficiently stoned and humming to herself as she gazed into the infinity of the ceiling. She felt weightless as she watched her right arm lift straight up into the air without any assistance from her. What followed was Rose rolling out of the bed and falling onto the floor. The impact of hitting the floor served to sober her up for a brief moment. "How did that happen?" she said out loud. She wondered if all marijuana was as strong as this stuff had been. Also, at hearing the thump when Rose hit the floor, Margie stuck her head in to see what on earth her daughter was doing. Rose just waved at her mom and smiled. Confused, Margie only shook her head and shut the door to Rose's room again.

The Ancient Paths

As if it had just now occurred to her, Rose crawled to the footlocker in the room and flipped the lid open. On top of everything was a square gift wrapped box. She picked it up, and giggling, she contemplated the package in her hand, and finally decided to open it.

Inside the box were two things, an envelope with "ROSE" written on it and another smaller box. Looking from one to the other, she tried to decide which one to open first. The box? The envelope? The box? The envelope? She wondered why it was so hard to decide. Must be that weed she had smoked. "Oh, what the heck!" she blurted out. Finally, she ripped open the envelope. Inside was a letter from her father. She had not been able to bring herself to look inside the package until today. Having all the resentment and bitterness toward her father that she had carried around with her all those years made it so difficult to even think of him now. And to think of him giving her a gift, well, that had been doubly hard for her. They had only received one child support check from him after they had returned to Nashville. She read the letter aloud:

"My dearest daughter Rose,

By the time you decide to read this, the cancer may have already taken me home to meet my maker.

I know in my heart that you, your brother and sisters all have reason to hate me. I tried to raise you guys in a manner that would be constructive, but a house in the country and a good school did not quite do the job. I know I failed all of you miserably.

I have made arrangements for my body to be cremated when my time has come. I only wish I could have received forgiveness from all of you before leaving this world. But, I will have to face my end, and can only hope that you will one day be able to forgive me. I hope that each of you can find it in your hearts to do that. Please forgive me, my children.

Your father,

Jose Rivera"

Tears streamed down Rose's cheeks. She didn't know if she was mad, sad or stoned or all three. "Forgive? How can I forgive what you did to me, Dad? And what you did to the others? How are we all supposed to forgive? Do we just…forget everything that happened?" That was, in fact, what they had tried to do- forget. Yet, somehow it had not been that easy.

Slowly reaching for the smaller box, she yanked the lid off and gasped. Inside was a purple stone ring with four small diamond studs mounted on a 14K gold band. It was an Alexandrite stone. Upon inspection of the ring, Rose found an inscription on the inside of the band. There, in cursive script, was the word "Sincerity."

***

"Are you sure this is okay?" Laurie was nervous about descending upon Tony without him knowing in advance that they were joining him.

"Of course it is. He's my brother, now quit worrying!"

The girls climbed the steps, and at the top of the steps, Rose found an antique foot locker she had not noticed before. She had one in her own room, but this one was new to her. She stopped long enough to look inside it and found all manner of merchandise—new silverware, china, blankets. She wondered where that had come from.

While Rose knew that her brother had visitors in his room that day, she was in fact surprised to find some of her schoolmates there in her brother's room. Sitting there in her brother's room were the fraternal twins, Edgar and Alex. Both guys were popular at school. They seemed to be as straight as anybody else at school, but then so did Rose. There, completing the group was also Jeff and Randy from her classes. Then there was some guy she had never seen before, a slightly more mature looking person with a nice looking moustache and pretty brown hair. When Rose called out, "Tony!" the guy in the moustache answered.

"Yeah, nobody likes a smart aleck," Rose blurted.

"Sorry, I thought you said Bo. That's my name. Guess I wasn't listening too closely." She knew he was just flirting with her though.

She also knew the answer before she even asked the question, "Hey, Tony, where did all that stuff come from in that locker? And whose nice looking Chevelle is that in the driveway?"

"The car is mine," Bo responded.

"Nice car. And exactly who *are you*?" Rose brazenly demanded.

"I'm their brother," he said, pointing to the twins. While Rose had just begun to grieve for Greg who had not left town yet, she found herself wondering how long she would need to grieve.

"No, I can't be thinking like that," she chided herself.

"But, Tony, where'd all that stuff in that locker come from?"

"Nick," was all he said, but she knew what he meant. Nick had been taking things from that warehouse where he worked again. That metal plate in his head had really messed him up according to everything her mom had told her about it.

Looking around at the group of men in her brother's room, Rose thought to herself, "So, what are they doing here?" But she knew. She could see. It was Tony. It wasn't her they had come to see. Tony was the cool head at school. Even rednecks who had once picked on Tony for being different had recently come to their home to see him. And now, seated in the middle of everyone was Tony, expertly putting cigarette rolling papers together and rolling a foot long joint. Rose sat down and pulled Laurie down next to her. Tony finished his rolling project and without a word handed it to Laurie.

Laurie felt like she was being dared. All eyes were on her, and she would be darned if she was going to back down. She may have been a lot of things, but chicken was not one of them. She took the foot long joint from Tony. To her, it looked to be about two or three feet long, not just one. She felt as if the circle of faces was closing in on her and found that she was sweating from nerves. Someone struck a match lighting the end of the stick, and Laurie exhaled a deep breath and then slowly inhaled.

So, to briefly summarize: We now have a houseful of four teenage siblings who have been reunited, who are largely unsupervised; we have a stepfather who has a metal plate in his head and is a kleptomaniac, and then there is the beautiful mother who works hard for the money as a waitress during the day. What can possibly go wrong here?

CHAPTER 22

To say that conflicts began to brew among the sibling group would be an understatement. While they had been away from everything that was familiar and in New York together, the kids had all felt like they were at least on the same side, probably because at the time each other was all they had had. Rose had helped to take care of her younger sisters because that was what she had to do. There had not been a mother there for any of them, only an occasional live in babysitter, which never seemed to last for long. Tony had tried to watch over them all as best he could, but he had been no match for their father's anger, aggression and brute strength. None of them had been.

Rose was so busy with her new friends and with being a teenager that she had lost sight of the fact her little sisters still needed her in some way. Even though they were no longer trapped in New York, her sisters had long looked to her to be there for them. Oddly enough, now that they were all finally living under one roof again and with their mom, they rarely saw one another.

Rose was caught up in her social life. She made good grades at school, she had a steady stream of suitors knocking at her door now that Greg had moved away, even though she was always turning down the offers for dates she received, and she had Laurie who was the best friend she could have hoped for who kept her busy. She had a habit of saying 'no' to her sisters whenever they would ask, "Can we come with you, Rose?" She was unaware of anything except what was going on in the world of Rose.

One day in the summertime as she sat swinging on the front porch, the mailman came by to deliver the mail, and among the bills was a letter to Rose from Greg. His number had come up for the draft. He would be going to Vietnam. "Oh no!" she screamed, not caring who heard her. Anna and Karen came running out of the house.

"What's wrong, Rose?" they asked together.

"Tell us what happened." Anna begged her.

"It's Greg. He's getting drafted into the army."

"Oh," both the younger sisters said.

"I may never get to see him again if he goes to Vietnam."

The sisters' hearts went out to her as they knelt beside her and embraced her. She put her arms around her younger sisters and was very appreciative that they were there for her at that moment.

The Ancient Paths

Anna was hesitant, but she said to speak her mind, "Sissie, I don't know much. I know you're older than me and all, but I think you need to think about dating someone else. Greg is away, you never see him, and now he will be going away for the Army. You might need to think about dating someone who's here."

Rose sniffed and nodded. She knew that Anna was making sense, but she would just feel so bad if she broke up with Greg at this time.

"That Bo guy is kind of cute, Sis. Why not date him?"

If her little sister only knew, the Bo guy was twenty-seven years old, ten years older than herself. Every week he was showing up at their home to see Tony, but would always ask Rose if she wanted to go for a ride in his Chevelle, and she would always tell him no.

That night, Bo showed up as usual to see her brother. On his way out, he stopped on the front porch where Rose was still sitting. She had spent the entire evening on the front porch swing just thinking. For some reason, she couldn't stand the claustrophobic feeling of being in the house that evening.

"Want to go for a ride, Rose?" he asked. Expecting her to say no as she always did, he didn't wait for an answer, but instead kept walking toward his car.

The Ancient Paths

"No, but I'll go for a walk with you," she whispered.

He stopped in his tracks. "I'm sorry. What?"

"I don't want to go for a ride with you right now, but if you want, we can go for a walk."

"Walk where, babe?"

She held out her hand to him, and he took it. "Come on. I have some new friends I'd like to introduce you to."

Bo had been to Vietnam. He had only recently returned from his tour of duty. He was twenty-seven and Rose was seventeen. While she had lived a lot of life for someone her age, she had not experienced it with someone who had seen the horrors of Vietnam. If the girl had only known what lay in store for her, she would have tucked her tail and ran for the hills that day.

It was dusk, so there was not much more daylight to be had, but fortunately, the home of Don and Marianne was located diagonally across the alley from the home of Rose and her family. The home which Don and Marianne occupied was a dirt stained rock house which did not appear to emit much light at all. As a matter of fact, it looked downright depressing.

"Who lives here?" Bo whispered.

"Just a couple I met last week. My sisters actually met them first, and they brought me over here to introduce me to them."

Rose knocked, and even though there was talking which was audible through the front door, no one immediately came to the door to greet them. Three minutes had passed and Rose became uncomfortable with the long wait and decided it was time for her to exit. Maybe they had come at a bad time.

As she was about to step off the porch, the front door was flung open wide, and there stood Marianne, with her long thick brown hair and her piercing green eyes which sparkled like gems. She was laughing, "Ha, ha. Um…hi! Will you come in?" she giggled again.

The house was practically barren of furniture. There were instead two bean bag chairs in the living room and a kitchen table with no chairs. That was all the furniture within sight, except for the stereo, which Don had cranked up to about three fourths of its maximum volume as he jumped around with his hands in his pocket, grinning as the song "Eight Miles High" by the Byrds blared in the background. Rose still could not get over the handsome face of Don with his dark brown eyes, dark hair and beard, and the exotic beauty of Marianne. But make no mistake about it, Ozzie and Harriet this couple definitely was not.

The Ancient Paths

"Hi," Don managed to verbalize as he waved at Rose and Tony while he continued jumping around. Marianne started jumping around with him. In the corner stood little Jessica, their daughter. She was as beautiful as both of her parents. Her eyes were pools of brown, and her face was exquisite. She was so beautiful, as a matter of fact, that it saddened Rose to see the child in her dirty little dress. It made her look like a third world child instead of a neighborhood child of Sylvan Park.

Finally, the music stopped and Don introduced himself to Bo.

"Hi, man. Welcome to our pad. I'm Don and this is my lady Marianne and our kid, Jessica."

Bo extended his hand. Don stared at it as if he had never had anyone offer to shake his hand before. Then he laughed and grabbed Bo's hand as he laughed again, "Oh yeah. Thanks, man. So, what's your name, man?"

"I'm Bo, Rose's...friend. So, are you guys new to the neighborhood? How long have y'all been married?"

Don's dark beard hid much of his facial expression, but it was obvious that he did not know what to say. And then a sudden moment of truth, as if it was something he had held back long enough, came gushing forth from his belly before he could realize what he had said.

"Naw, man. We aren't married. We've been together for about three years. We met in Florida when I was running from the law. I was a deserter. I refused to go to Vietnam."

Rose's jaw fell open. So did Bo's. Bo had done his time in Nam, and he still had the nightmares to prove it. He understood someone not wanting to go, but it always got his ire up.

As for Rose, oh boy, she just learned a little more than she cared to know! In spite of the rocky start to the introductions, before the evening was over, Don and Bo had exchanged phone numbers. Rose had a creepy feeling though, and was not so sure she was okay with that.

***

In the beginning, getting to know Bo was kind of fun. He had the money to take Rose out to movies and to dinner, things she hadn't really done before. Before Bo, it had always been a soda fountain drink at Kuhn's or the Spy teen dance which was held at McCabe Park on the weekends.

Now, sometimes she and Bo would go for day trips on the weekend. Rose's parents were concerned. They didn't know how old Bo was, but they knew for a fact he was somewhat older than Rose; yet, simultaneously, they realized that she would soon be eighteen and was going to do what she wanted to, whether they approved or not.

The Ancient Paths

The real problem though was in the fact that Rose had never officially broken up with Greg. Margie knew that Rose was young and wanted to be with someone who adored her, but she also knew that not doing things the right way could come back to haunt Rose.

One evening over dinner, Bo casually mentioned to Rose, "You know your neighbors Marianne and Don that you introduced me to a few weeks ago?" He put down his fork and looked at her squarely in the eyes, defiant in his gaze, but still trying to gauge his words "Well, I slept with her." So much for gauging his words.

"You what! You slept with who?!" Her eyes glared at him and pierced right through his soul.

"Marianne. I slept with her." He looked her squarely in the eye, as if he were being magnanimous by telling her. "Um...yeah. Seems that Don is pretty violent, not been treating her right..."

"So what? So, you were just there and more than willing to help her out and 'treat her right'? I trusted you. I introduced you to what I thought were my friends, and the first chance you get, you sleep with her! You moron! What did Don think about that?"

He took a deep breath. "Well...seems that they have an open relationship. They are both free to have sex with anyone else they want."

So, as abruptly as that, her ideal fairy tale romance with an older man ended. Rose leaned across the table and hissed at Bo, "Well, you know? I am not them, and I do not want an open relationship, you jerk." She grabbed her drink, and standing up, she threw it in his face, then she stormed out to call her parents. "I should have known better," she kept repeating to herself. "I should have known better."

She would have to tell Greg that they were through too. No matter how she cut it, sliced it or diced it, she had definitely cheated on him. So, in a sense, what she had done was no better than what Bo had just confessed to. She also found herself wondering where she had gotten such a bad temper.

CHAPTER 23

Rose's life became like a series of dots. Because she had an older brother, because she had dated an older man, and because some of her acquaintances such as Marianne and Don were older, some of her other friends and acquaintances were also older. If you connected the dots, it seemed that all of her friends were somehow connected. Rose decided to call Dabney and Tim. They were friends she had recently met via Don and Marianne, before Bo had broken the news to her that he had slept with Marianne. Even though she was horribly upset after Bo admitted to sleeping with Marianne, and she knew she was definitely through with Marianne and Don, Rose still felt close to Dabney and Tim. She hoped to find some consolation through them after the pain she had just experienced as a result of Bo's betrayal.

She decided to call them up and ask if it was alright for her to come over and visit.

"Yeah, of course," said Dabney, "come on over and spend the night. We have some new friends we would like for you to meet anyway."

"Well, okay. I'll see if I can get a ride over there." Rose was a little wary since she had never spent the night at their home, but she wanted somewhere to go where she would not have to just sit home and think.

Nick and Margie drove Rose to Dabney and Tim's that evening. Try as they may, it was difficult to ignore the fact that there was a blue school bus in the driveway. "What in the world!" remarked Margie. "Whose bus is that anyway, Rose?"

"Honestly, Mom, I don't know. I've only been here once before. I'll call you guys when I'm ready to come home. Thank you for the ride." She kissed Margie on the cheek and hopped out of the car.

Upon her entrance through the kitchen door of the 'green house', which was the name that had been designated for the home of Dabney and Tim, there was a significant number of strange people filling the home of her friends that day. Rose had noticed the license plate was from CALIFORNIA, but who the heck were these folks?

Running up to Rose and grabbing her, Dabney lifted her off the ground, and gave her a bear hug, swinging her around. Dabney was a beautiful woman with short dark hair, electric hazel eyes and an exuberant personality which was contagious. She was a singer and performer for a living, so she was a natural with people. "Ah! Look at you, little Rose. Come on in and meet our new friends. These guys just came in last week from California. They are the Caravan."

In every room there existed every sort of long, lanky, bearded, unbathed, long haired hippie man or woman you could imagine. There were small children running around in underwear only, slapping each other, squealing and pulling hair. It was utter chaos.

Within The Caravan which was a religious cult group, the group's leader believed that one man's wife was every man's wife, and one man's child was everyone else's child. In short, The Caravan was a commune which had just arrived in the small city of Nashville from California. Rose had seen the short story on the news about the busloads of the commune which had arrived in town within the past week, now here some of them were in the flesh.

Rose was not so sure she should have come. She had to admit to herself that she felt lost, alone and lonely there. She didn't feel like she exactly fit in with this crowd, as much as she liked Dabney and Tim.

Dabney told Rose, "We don't have any weed to smoke, but these guys have got some peyote buttons, which they boil down and drink in a tea. They have something called an Om, Rose, which is kind of like their prayer. Do you want to drink some of the tea and participate in the Om?" What choice did she have? There was nowhere for her to run, and besides, if she could just get high, she might forget about how lousy she was feeling.

After the peyote buttons had been boiled and the tea prepared, a large sheet was laid on the floor and everyone in the room sat around the perimeter of the sheet with legs crossed. The tea was drunk, and then everyone began to chant, making the sound "Om." Rose was not sure what the heck Om meant, but she went along with everyone. Maybe it was the peyote, maybe it was her imagination, but at one point, Rose could have sworn it felt like they had transcended their bodies and were in a place where they all were one. She had never felt anything quite like that before. As soon as the Om ended, the euphoria was lost to the sounds of everyday life once again, babies crying, children fighting, and husbands and wives arguing. In other words, Rose went straight from Om to what she thought could possibly be the sounds of hell.

CHAPTER 24

Just how gullible do you have to be to be taken advantage of? The answer is "as gullible as Rose." Oh yeah. Rose had set Greg free, even though she hated herself for it. She had learned that she could not be faithful to him while he was so far away. Besides, she reasoned with herself, she was still so young. And when Bo came begging back to be in her good graces, she caved. She asked herself, "How can I say no?" She had given herself to him, and she was hooked. Besides, she was bored with boys her own age now. She did not know the meaning of the word boundaries. Nor did she think about the fact that she had been unwilling to forgive her father, even on his death bed. It hurt too much to even think of her father now.

Bo was a policeman with the Metro Police Department and he had loved his job. And when he was given the choice to cut his hair or lose his job, he opted for losing his job. After Vietnam, he was all about rebelling and not conforming to the will of the man, so to speak.

With all that time on his hands now, Bo did not want to stay out of trouble. When Rose arrived at Bo's apartment after school and walked in on him with yet another woman whom she had never met in his bed, she was enraged. "Do not, I repeat, do not EVER talk to me again!" And with that, she was out the door, slamming it so hard that it broke the hinges. How could she have been so deceived? But boy, did it ever hurt.

The next day was the last day of school before summer break. Laurie caught up with Rose at her locker. "Rose, did you see the news this morning?"

"No, I didn't. Why?"

"Rose, Bo is all over the news. He got busted last night!"

Rose was blindsided. "What are you talking about? I was there yesterday. Only for a minute though. I was so angry I couldn't see straight. He was in bed with yet another chick! I'm through with that butthead. I should have never let Greg go. He was the one good thing in my life."

Laurie looked around, then lowered her eyes to the ground, "Rose, I have to tell you, girl. You need to let Greg go too. He wasn't who you thought he was either."

"What! What do you mean? So, if he wasn't who I thought he was...who the heck was he?" By now, she was beginning to wonder if she was even the person she had thought she was.

"I don't know, Rose. I guess he was a very human young man with flaws like all of us. Remember that chick named Torie that used to live next door to you? Well, apparently, he was messing around with her when you and him started going together. It took him awhile to cut it off with her. I heard this through the grapevine today. From what I hear, Torie's still in touch with some kids here at school, and she told them." She hurt to see Rose hurting so badly.

Rose was thrown off balance with all of the news today. "So, what is this? All of my guys are sleeping with all my neighbors or something? I can't believe Greg would have done that!"

"I'm so sorry, Rose. I know you really respected and loved Greg, but nothing is ever easy, is it? Now, about Bo—he apparently had about twenty pounds of weed at his place when they busted him, Rose."

Rose was laughing, crying and shaking her head at the same time now, and she spoke in between the tears and laughter while trying to dry her eyes. "Good grief. I wonder if it was at his place when I was there yesterday. What time was it when all this happened, I wonder."

"I think they said about six p.m."

"Geez! I hadn't been gone for too long then, maybe like twenty minutes. Good grief. That was a close call. Man, am I glad I wasn't there when this stuff went down. That idiot!"

That evening when Bo called Rose, she was livid. "I hate you, Bo. You are nothing but a lowdown, lying sack of dog poop. Who the heck was that girl? And why didn't you tell me you had bales of weed in your home? Are you out of your mind? Why are you even calling me?"

"I'm sorry, Rose. I never meant to hurt you. I love you, but I love her too. Her name is Lydia. She is a good person, and I want you and her to be friends after I leave. I want you to ride with me, Lydia, Tim and Dabney. They are going to get me out of town, and they will bring you back home. Remember this, I want you and Lydia to get to know each other."

"For Pete's sake, Bo! Are you just absolutely insane? You want me to go out of town with you and your other girlfriend to take you out of town. I don't know if I want to be friends with another girl you say you love! Who in the heck do you think you are anyway?"

"You'll be able to go. You know your mother will let you do anything you want. She loves you guys so much, she doesn't know how to say no to you."

"Yeah, you're right. Unfortunately, it looks like that's a trait I've inherited."

CHAPTER 25

Rose had been gone for a week. She had done it. She made that long bizarre road trip with Bo, Lydia, Tim and Dabney. How she got through it, she didn't even know. She only knew she was tired, stressed to the max, hacked off and had road hypnosis. California is a long way from Nashville, and to make the trip with a guy you both love and hate plus his other girlfriend, well that was just something else. She hoped she would never have to think about or see Bo again. Good riddance, he was gone. She did not need any more heartache in her life, ever again. The weird thing was though, she had actually liked Lydia. She wasn't sure about wanting to be her friend though. "This is one experience I will never talk about again," she silently vowed.

Exhausted, she climbed the same steps to the same porch she had seen practically every day for the past several years. She closed her eyes, worn and weary. "Oh please, let my life get back to normal," she said, to whom she was not sure. So when she grabbed the handle to the screen door and found it to be locked, she lost the last bit of patience in her body, and banged on the door, shouting, "Somebody let me in!"

She waited to see if Anna or Karen would come and unlock the door, but the person who greeted her was no one she had ever seen before. Tosha was a grown woman who looked to be one to two years older that Rose; yet, her outward appearance was much like that of a little girl. Her hair was long, thick, wavy, sandy colored, and she wore a scarf which held much of her bangs and hair on her left side in place. She had large dark brown eyes about the size of quarters, and her fingernails were long and painted black. Underneath her arm she carried a huge Raggedy Anna doll. Her blue jeans were rolled up almost to the knees, and on her feet was a pair of brown leather boots that laced up the front with black shoestrings. She was peculiar looking to say the least. "You've got to be kidding! She looks like a bad dream," Rose thought.

Without saying a word, Tosha unlocked the door, and the two stood facing each other, each refusing to utter the first words. Finally, Rose in her anger and frustration yelled out to whomever was within hearing range, "Who the heck is this?"

Margie came running into the living room. "What's wrong, sweetie?"

Rose was close to panic mode now. She had just come off the road from a very traumatic experience with that jerk of a boyfriend Bo and his other love, and having to come home and face such an odd character before even stepping into her home was a bit more than Rose felt like coping with at the moment.

Rose was visibly shaken by Tosha's appearance, and Tosha knew it. She smirked at Rose and was obviously amused and getting some sort of satisfaction at the look of confusion on Rose's face. With her long black fingernails, Tosha waved hello to Rose. "You pretty," she said. So, the girl was an odd bird, to say the least.

Rose was astounded and incensed. "What the...who *is* she though?!" Rose demanded looking at her mother again.

"Well, honey, she's your brother's new girlfriend."

Rose was speechless for once. "Oh my goodness!" she thought to herself. "What has happened to my big brother? I know. This is somehow my fault! Did everyone lose their minds in the week that I was gone?"

Anna and Karen came running into the living room at that moment and were all excited to see Rose, jumping up and down, hugging her, then just as abruptly turned their focus toward Tosha. "Rose," Anna gushed, "isn't Tosha cool? Look at her? She's living with us now!"

Rose was beyond frustrated. She was downright incensed. There was just something about this strange girl in her home that Rose could not get past. She stood scratching her head as she tried to makes sense of everything she was hearing. "I'm gone for one week, and we have a boarder?" she blurted out, not making any false attempts at being tactful. She stood trembling, and everyone could see she was upset. Margie, Anna and Karen all held their breath. After a moment of deep breathing, she collected herself and finally calmed down long enough to speak civilly to Tosha. After scrutinizing Tosha's face a moment longer, Rose said softly, "You know, Tosha, there is something really familiar about you."

Tosha drew closer until she was practically in Rose's face. "Yeah, you too, Rose. I feel like…like I'm looking through the looking glass and seeing myself."

Rose was caught up in Tosha's hypnotic gaze. Abruptly, she realized that her skin was crawling. She also realized that the things she saw in Tosha's eyes were, well, let's say they weren't quite normal, or more precisely, they weren't human.

Later, Margie would tell Rose, "Tony says that things are bad at Tosha's home. She doesn't feel loved there, and she wants to be here where she feels loved."

"Well, la-dee-dah!" was all Rose could think.

***

Anna and Karen got a big kick out of 'playing' with Tosha. Rose could not help but observe the way that her little sisters had taken to their new housemate. She couldn't believe her parents had actually allowed Tony to bring his girlfriend into their home to live with him. What was going on here? Had they all taken leave of their senses for real? Rose was pretty certain that Nick was not okay with that arrangement, and yet he had allowed it.

Rose would soon learn that Tosha was actually the offspring of a wealthy pharmacy entrepreneur, and her family was affluent and rather eccentric. Tosha did not need a place to live, she just wanted to live with Tony. Tosha began transferring hoards of clothing from her closet into the upstairs bedroom that she shared with Tony now. And every time Rose saw her bringing in more clothes, she got angry all over again.

As Anna paraded around the house in a dress from Tosha's latest installment of clothing she had provided to the girls, Rose overheard Tosha say, "You are me now, and I feel so you."

"What in the bloody heck is going on here?" Rose barged in and hissed at Tosha. "What are you doing to my sisters?"

"Why, nothing Rose. We are 'playing' dress up. That's all."

"Well, since when do young teens 'play' dress up, anyway?" Rose demanded.

"Rose, don't worry. It's all in fun. Here, take my doll, Belladonna. You'll see. We're just playing. You must understand, Rose, darling. Your family is not earthlings, really you aren't. None of you are earthlings."

"I will not take your stupid doll!" And with that, Rose snatched the doll out of Tosha's hands, threw it against the wall and stormed out.

Anna and Karen didn't flinch. They remained in their spot and continued playing their game of dress up with Tosha. They both now wore blue jeans rolled up to their knees, scarves in their hair, socks up to their knees and carried dolls under their arms. What was going on with her sisters? They were actually becoming like a couple of little Tosha's. As a matter of fact, Rose was beginning to feel like she had stepped into the darn Twilight Zone.

Laurie called Rose that afternoon. "Rose, where have you been? You've all but disappeared since that weird chick, what's her name, moved in over there. Are you alright?"

"I don't know, Laurie. It's just that there used to always be someone here. Some of our friends were always dropping by to hang out. Now, it's like, no one's here anymore…no one but us. You don't ever come here either. That may be one reason you haven't seen me." She could sense the silence on the other end of the phone.

"It's not that I don't love you, girl. You know that. You're my best friend. But, that girl is bad news. I feel it. Maybe me and your bud Arlo can come get you out of the house here soon. Okay?"

"Sure."

Arlo was gorgeous with tall, slender limbs, sandy blond hair, brown eyes and finely chiseled features...and rich to boot. Rose knew he liked her, but she was so leery of trusting another male right now. And yet, when he showed up by himself to see if she wanted to go for a ride, she didn't hesitate. "Anything to get me out of here," she reasoned with herself. Arlo couldn't help but notice Tosha as she silently opened up the door that lead to Tony's room and disappeared.

"I've heard about that girl, and I have to agree, she's pretty freakin' weird. Just because she didn't talk, it doesn't mean I didn't see her. She acts like she thinks she's invisible or something. Gives me the creeps."

"You know, my brother moved her in here to live with us, and now I never see him. She's always here, and he's always gone. Not only that, I can't stand her."

"Come on, let's get out of here." Arlo held out his hand to her, and she gladly let him lead her out of the house.

The Ancient Paths

"Where are we going, Arlo?"

"To visit a jeweler friend of mine."

The ring that Arlo purchased for Rose was unique since she had never seen one quite like it. It was a stainless steel ring carved into the shape of a bumble bee. What made it most unique was that one of its wings was broken. Since the jeweler, Maria, had just returned from Europe where she had had some measure of success in selling her wares, Rose was honored to have one of her masterpieces, even if it had a broken wing. That made it even more special to Rose somehow, as there were times when she knew she must be like the bee whose wing had been clipped.

That evening when Rose returned home, she decided to stay outside on the swing for a while. It was her favorite place to be, especially when she didn't feel like coping with everything else, which seemed to be more and more frequently as of late. She wasn't ready to go inside the house to that madness quite yet, but as fate would have it, Tosha, Anna and Karen came running outside to greet her. Tosha was the first to speak, "Hi, Rose. I hope you had fun with your friend today."

"Yes, I did. Thank you."

Anna was the first to notice the bumble bee ring. "Sissy, where did you get that ring? And what is it?"

"Well, it's a bumble bee with a broken wing, Anna. See?" She held the ring up for everyone to inspect.

Since Anna had Rose's attention, Rose did not take note right away that Tosha was stroking her hair. She didn't know why, but for no apparent reason, Rose was all of a sudden sleepy.

"Look here, Rose," Tosha spoke in a soothing tone which was mesmerizing. "Look at *my* ring." She held up a crystal ring, and when Rose looked into it, it was like a prism, and its depth unfolded a hundred times over and it went on forever. Rose was in a trance. She felt trapped inside that prism. "Let's exchange rings for a while, Rose."

"Okay," Rose said, not knowing why she said it. With that, Tosha slipped the bumble bee ring off of Rose's finger and slipped her crystal ring onto Rose's finger.

Tosha spoke in her soothing manner to Rose, stroking her hair, the sound of her voice lulling Rose further into a trance. "That's right, Rose. I'm your real friend. All those other people, they weren't your friends. From now on, I am your best friend." The sisters who had observed all that took place did not try to intervene. They were unaware of any wrong doings since they themselves were under

Tosha's spell. The sisters were all living some sort of kooky fantasy and Tosha was directing this fantasy. "Come on, let me give you a manicure, Rose. You need to have those nails trimmed," and with that, she reached to stroke Rose's hair again, but instead managed to wrap her fingers around several strands of hair and yanked, which broke the magic of the moment.

"What the heck!" Rose snapped at her, rubbing her head where the strand of hair had been yanked out suddenly. Rose was very tender headed.

"You were just asking me to give you a manicure. Come on."

While Rose's body obeyed, something inside her screamed, "Help!"

CHAPTER 26

It was a fact, Anna and Karen adored Tosha. Rose could clearly see that, and she could not help but feel a twinge of jealousy. While she had for the most part ignored the lives of her younger sisters when she had been busy with Greg or Bo, Laurie or Arlo, she now had the time to spend with her sisters, and they were not so interested in spending time with her. They were instead focused on their new friend. So, when Anna approached Rose and asked, "Rose, do you want to go to Tosha's parents with us today and swim?" against her own best judgment, she said, "Sure, whatever you want to do, Anna."

Transportation was not a problem, since Tosha's parents were wealthy enough to buy her a car. The ride to their home was a blur to Rose. Even though Tosha had hypnotized Rose long enough to talk her out of her ring that night, Rose had regained her senses; and yet, there was something about Tosha which overpowered Rose. In Tosha's presence, Rose felt small and insignificant, even helpless.

To say this was a motley looking crew was an understatement. Tosha led the pack with her long grey choir robe, black boots and hair pulled up in a ponytail secured with a scarf; as usual, Anna wore her rolled up blue jeans, scarf in her hair, tennis shoes and bells tied to her

221

belt loop; Karen looked like a life size doll in a pink dress with large white polka dots, complete with black patent leather shoes; Rose brought up the rear in her tie dyed shirt and patchwork blue jeans and sandals. But, when Tosha rang the doorbell and her mother opened the door, her mom didn't seem the least bit surprised.

While Tosha's mother Sue and she looked nothing alike, the sound of their voices was very much alike, and together were enough to get on Rose's nerves. It was eleven o'clock in the morning, and Sue was already sipping on a mixed drink. "Hi, Mommy," Tosha said, greeting her mom with an air kiss. Funny, but to Rose that seemed a bit pretentious for a mother and daughter. "Is it okay if we swim today?"

"Sure, sweetie, but where have you been?" Rose gritted her teeth when she heard Sue talk because it felt like she was in a room with two Tosha's instead of one. Good Lord, how was it possible that there were two who sounded so much alike?

"Mommy, come on! You know I'm living at Tony's home now, and these are Tony's sisters. The first and prettiest of these girls is Anna. Take a bow Anna." Speechless, Anna gave a quick curtsey instead of bowing. Tosha continued on, "The pretty little doll here is Karen. And last but not least, this ugly duckling is Rose. Snap out of it, Rose. You mustn't act the least bit spacey." Rose's eyes were literally bulging out of their sockets by now. She was ready to not only kick that girl's butt, she wanted to tear her from limb to limb. But she was not on her home turf. She was in Tosha's mother's home. Why had she agreed to come on this looney tunes trip with this crazy chick?

The swimming pool was just outside the kitchen door. Tosha remained in the house with her mother while the girls made their way to the pool.

No, Tosha was not the poor little thing that she had first made herself out to be. Rose knew it for a fact now. Tosha's mom was somewhat of a spoiled housewife and a lush, but Tosha was definitely Rose's worst nightmare come to life. How could her brother ever have fallen for such a dark soul?

Even though the temperature outside was warm, it felt unexplainably cold standing there in the backyard of Tosha's family home. Rose shivered. Her sisters quickly removed their clothes to reveal their swimsuits and waded into the water. "Come on, Rose!" they encouraged her. She was slow to respond. She could not shake a feeling of heaviness, weariness and loneliness. She did not know where she fit into this picture anymore, and she never felt happy nowadays.

After the girls had exhausted themselves in the water, Tosha escorted them to her room on the second level of the house. Upon entering the room, Rose at once sensed the presence of that same coldness she had felt out by the pool, only now it was more pronounced. There was also a darkness whose presence was so powerful that it took her breath. She did a quick survey of the décor and decided that this place looked more like a mausoleum than a bedroom that belonged to what should be a happy, vibrant young woman.

The room was small and narrow. The window was covered with ivory colored lace curtains, and the sunlight filtered through the dismally lit room, kissing the black rose in the vase on top of the lace covered round table which was located next to the window. From the black rose, the light swept across the carpet and made its way to the life-like ceramic doll on the bed. The doll was beautiful but terrifying in its human likeness. Her perfectly shaped lips and perfect blond hair were enhanced even more by the fact that this doll was an absolute replica of Tosha. Dressed in a grey robe with its hair pulled into a pony tail with a scarf, the doll held the attention of all the sisters. It was as though time had stopped in this room, and a spirit of death permeated the space.

"What the devil is this place?" Rose whispered. She was about to jump out of her skin.

"It used to be my little brother's room. He died when he was a baby. I moved in here after he died," Tosha explained in that same loud voice that always irritated Rose.

The Ancient Paths

"Geez! No wonder she wants to live somewhere else," Rose silently mused.

"Girls, you can change in here. Check out my closet and see if there is something you want to wear. You can wear anything in there." Anna and Karen clapped their delicate young hands together and squealed in delight as though they were small children once again. In Rose's estimation, when they were with Tosha, her sisters actually did seem like such children. Rose alone did not react to Tosha's declaration of generosity.

"Thank you, my lady Tosha," Anna responded, rather dramatically. Rose was dumbstruck. What did her sister just say? And since *when* did Anna start talking like something out of Victorian times?!

CHAPTER 27

Each day was a new adventure for Rose. She often wondered if she was destined to simply float through life. She was dependent on her parents for food and a place to stay. She was dependent on her parents for rides. At times, she even turned to Tosha for rides, which she loathed doing. Tony was working somewhere nowadays, but Rose had no idea where, and he was still never around. So, she knew she needn't bother asking him for rides.

She was still seventeen, almost eighteen and would graduate from high school next year. But, for right now, Laurie's mom and dad had given her a car for her birthday, so Rose and Laurie were able to hang out together without having to bum rides. Maybe Laurie's parents could buy her a car, but if Rose wanted a car, she would definitely have to work for it. She knew her mom and stepdad wanted her to get a job and work, and maybe she should, she thought. But she didn't feel ready for it yet.

It was the beginning of the weekend and a hot, muggy summer night. Arlo had called to invite Rose to a party that evening. She called Laurie to see if she was game. "Well, heck yeah, girl. That's why I have this car now, so we can have some fun."

The Ancient Paths

Even though Arlo had given Rose the address, she was not familiar with where this house was located. Laurie on the other hand, had been there once before, and when Laurie pulled into the long, winding driveway on Hillsboro Road, Rose could not believe her eyes. The place was a mansion. The entire driveway was lit all the way to the house. The big granite rocks of the home's exterior were well lit with outdoor lighting as well. It looked like something out of *The Great Gatsby.*

Music was blaring through the door before they even got inside T.J.'s home. The foyer alone was as big as Rose's living room. She had never been in such a house before. From room to room they wandered. The curtains, the artwork, the furniture, the carpet, the paint colors, everything was picture perfect and expensively designed. Groups of teens and young adults were socializing everywhere Rose looked, and she found herself wondering where the parents of this house were. Some people were in small groups, talking quietly. Others were in larger groups, passing joints around in a circle. In the kitchen, people mixed drinks and milled about, making small talk. Some were taking turns snorting cocaine out of a coke spoon.

When a Quaalude and cocaine were offered to Rose, she thought, "Why not?" She turned to look for Laurie, but Laurie had already wandered off to another room. Rose didn't know what Quaalude or coke was, but she was about to find out. The young man who had offered her the drugs was smoking a joint, and he blew the smoke in her face after she had sniffed the cocaine up her nose. "Wow!" she was experiencing a head rush after that toot of coke. The weed must have been good too, because she copped a buzz without even smoking it. But, these were rich kids here, and they apparently could afford the best stuff. Laughing, she remembered that they had not introduced themselves yet. "I'm Rose, so what's your name?"

Rose was finally noticing just how handsome this guy was. He was tanned, had dark brown hair, blue eyes and high cheekbones. He almost looked like he could be a relative of hers, except for the fact that she had never laid eyes on him in her life, and very few of her relatives had blue eyes. There were a few on her mother's side of the family, but not many. She didn't know about her dad's side.

"Hi, I'm Roland." He held out his hand which Rose gladly accepted. "I'm not really as connected with some of these folks as others are. I guess you could say I'm an outsider. In other words, I'm not one of the brat pack. I'm a camera operator and I actually have to work for a living." His smile was beautiful with those crazy blue eyes and dark tanned skin.

Rose came out of her fog enough to realize that she was sweating and the air was stagnant. Why was it so hot in this big, beautiful mansion? These people, whoever these people were, must have more than enough money to run the air. "If you're going to live in a mansion, at least have enough money to run the stupid air conditioner," she thought.

After spending some time in the kitchen chatting with various people she didn't know, Rose finally remembered that it was Arlo who had invited her here, and she wondered exactly where he might be. Besides, she wanted to ask him if someone would turn on the freakin' air conditioner. She stumbled out of the kitchen, and she didn't understand why she was stumbling. "Oh yeah, I took that Quaalude thingie. Oh my gosh, oh yeah…the coke too. Ah!! Oh, shh!" she giggled aloud to no one in particular. She was feeling a little more relaxed than she was used to.

After bumping into several people while trying to find her way around the massive home, and eventually ending up in a small sitting room, she found herself face to face with someone she didn't quite recognize. He didn't have on his glasses, so Arlo was flying under the radar that night. His sandy blond head was laid back on the sofa, and his long, slender legs in their blue jeans were crossed; he was wearing a pair of clogs, and he held a glass of white wine he had been sipping on. A young woman with long brown hair sat beside him, talking to him, trying to hold his attention. But, when Arlo spotted Rose and smiled at her, the woman sitting beside him recognized that his interest was not in her, so she quietly removed herself.

"Wow. He's gorgeous." Rose had never really noticed how well put together Arlo actually was. He locked gazes with her and smiled, patting the empty seat beside him. Even though Arlo was looking directly at her, she had to look around to make sure he wasn't motioning to someone else. She didn't see another person in the room in his line of vision, so she pointed at herself and mouthed, "Me?" He nodded and patted the vacated space on the sofa again. She quietly crossed the room and sat down beside him.

"Are you having a good time, Rose?"

"Sure. But, I need to look for Laurie right now. I'll see you in a little while. Okay?" She had already forgotten to ask him about the air conditioner. Her thoughts were all over the board.

She didn't see Laurie anywhere, so she knew she was on her own...for about two minutes. She didn't have to look long, because Laurie seemingly emerged from nowhere.

"Gosh, Rose. This place is insanely hot. The air conditioner's broke, and T.J.'s parents are in Europe! Air won't be fixed until they get back. But, guess what!"

Rose was afraid to answer. "What?"

Laurie talked softer and lower, "Don't tell anybody, but there is a giant swimming pool out there. We passed it on the way in."

"There's no swimming pool out there. I didn't see it." Rose figured if she didn't see it, it must not be there.

"It's there alright. We didn't notice it because it was so far away from the main drive. But, let's sneak out there and go skinny dipping."

"Well, alright Laurie, if you don't tell anybody. "

"Don't worry, I won't. We'll just sneak out this door and not say a word.

Once they reached the pool, Rose and Laurie quickly stripped down to their birthday suits and quietly made their way into the pool. The tepid water was welcome on Rose's hot and thirsty skin. They did not want to draw any attention to themselves.

Too late though. Suddenly, there were naked bodies flying into the pool from every direction and bombarding Rose and Laurie with water in their faces.

"Laurie, I thought you said you weren't going to tell anybody."

"You saw me and you know I didn't, Rose. They must have seen us slip out here."

Without any warning, Rose felt a hand on her left ankle as she was pulled under the water in the night. The grip on her foot was strong. She struggled to free herself, and when she surfaced, she was face to face with Arlo.

"Arlo! Hey. I was going to look for you again, but ended up out here instead."

"This was a good idea though, Rose. Everybody got cooled off. Have you had the tour of the house yet?

"No."

"Can I give you the tour?"

"Um…okay. But, let me tell Laurie."

During her conversation with Arlo, Laurie had slipped away. She was always doing that. But Rose easily found her friend talking to a small group of other young people in the water. "Hey, Laurie, Arlo wants to give me the tour of the house."

Laurie thumped Rose on her noggin. "Doe bird, he wants to get you in the bed."

"What?"

"You heard me. Arlo's not going to give you any tour. He just wants to get you in the sack, sweetie."

"So, how do you know so much about Arlo, Laurie?"

"I've known Arlo since we were kids, remember?"

"Well, whatever. I'm going to let him give me the tour."

Rose got the tour alright—the tour of the master bedroom. When Laurie next caught up with Rose, Arlo was dressing himself, and Rose was in the bed high as a kite. "Rose, do you need any help getting dressed, sweetie?"

Every inhibition had gone out of Rose's body with the Quaalude and the cocaine that night. She was as limber as a cooked spaghetti noodle. "Yes, I can probably use some help...Lau-rie," Rose giggled.

Laurie scrounged around for Rose's clothing and Arlo leaned over and kissed Rose goodbye as her friend dressed her. "Let's talk soon," he said.

"You were right, Laurie. I'm sorry," Rose reverted from the giggles to choking back tears, feeling a bit gullible and stupid when Arlo had left the room. "I am so naive."

"It's okay, Rose. Let's just get out of here and get home."

Rose slumped into the passenger's seat, leaned her head on the head rest and closed her eyes. As Laurie pulled out of the drive way, she turned the radio on low. Rose hummed softly to herself and was about ready to doze off, when suddenly, something happened which Rose had thought only existed in sci-fi films. If she had had to put it into words, she would have said that it felt like the presence of another being, trying to climb into her body and take it over. It actually hurt her and she cried out in horror. "Laurie. Help me!" Her faced was distorted in fear and agony.

"What is it, Rose? What's going on?" Laurie could see that something definitely unnatural was going on with her friend.

Rose was sobbing. "You have to help me, Laurie. There is something evil here, and it's trying to get inside of me." Rose was having to resist this entity with every ounce of strength in her body, soul and mind.

Laurie was astonished. "Rose, stop it. You're scaring me! Maybe you just did too many ludes and too much coke tonight, girl."

"No, Laurie. I swear. I can't move my arms or my legs, and there is something crawling into my body! Just close your eyes, Laurie, and you will feel it, and you'll know what this is." Her face contorted again and Laurie was half out of her mind with fright.

Laurie's mind was furiously at work. Cruising down the road, she closed her eyes for a second or two and then opened wide. "It's her. I know it's her. I can feel her presence here with us now. Oh my God! You know, it took me awhile to believe you when you said that she was practicing witchcraft. But even then, I thought it was harmless. I guess I was mistaken. I'm so sorry I didn't take you more serious, Rose."

"Oh my God," said Rose. "You're right. It's definitely her. She's always saying that she feels so much like me, or that she feels like she's jumping through the looking glass and seeing herself when she looks in my eyes. Well, she is not me, and I am not her, and she can't have this body to inhabit!"

"Rose, aren't you wearing her ring?"

Rose had entirely forgotten by now that she still had Tosha's ring in her possession, and that Tosha had hers. She looked down at her hand, and there was the ring, glowing, as if it had come to life. "Laurie, pull over somewhere, anywhere. We have to get rid of this thing."

Laurie drove until she found an isolated spot off the main drag and pulled over. She reached over and pulled the ring off of Rose's finger, and at once, Rose was able to move her legs and arms again. "Oh my gosh, Laurie," she sobbed.

"Ooh, take this...this thing, Rose. I don't want to touch it."

Rose didn't want it either, but she knew what she had to do. "Hand it here and follow me." It was dark and the two girls were very aware of the fact that they were alone.

Rose found a lot full of healthy looking trees. She handed the ring back to Laurie. "Laurie, hold it one more time, please." Laurie nodded and Rose put the ring back in her hand, then turned and with her own hands, dug a hole about five inches deep beside one of the trees, took the ring back from Laurie and buried it there. "Let's forget this place ever existed. We'll never find this tree again, so that ring is gone for good. Adios." The girls rushed to get back in the car before any new danger might emerge from the dark of the night.

Laurie dropped off Rose at her home that night. "Are you going to be okay, Rose? Do you need me to come in?"

"No. Thanks, girlfriend, but I'm fine." She gave Laurie a big hug. Laurie knew her so well.

Once she was sure Rose had made it safely inside the door, Laurie was gone.

The Ancient Paths

Everyone was asleep, as it was late by then. Rose made sure to close the front door quietly so as not to wake anyone. Tiptoeing toward her room, she saw a light coming from in there. That was odd. She knew her sisters would not be in her room this late; they would be fast asleep. There was no noise coming for the direction of her room, only light. The door was barely cracked open, and when Rose peeked in, she gasped, and then slapped her hand over her mouth. There, sitting on her bed was Tosha. Everything suddenly came into clear focus for Rose when she saw that Tosha had Rose's dark haired collectible doll and was sticking pins in it. Rose looked down at her hands and remembered Tosha's words that today, "You were just asking me to give you a manicure." Her fingernails which Tosha had cut during her manicure were laid out in a circle around the doll, no less. In addition, Rose recognized her own long black strands of hair that Tosha had pulled from her head and was now wrapping around the bumble bee of her bumble bee ring. The words which came out of Tosha's mouth were barely audible, but Rose knew what they meant. She quietly turned and walked back outside to the front porch and sat on the swing, waiting for daylight. Rose said under her breath, "Sometimes, I just wish she would die."

CHAPTER 28

Rose had not seen her grandmother in what now seemed like years. She had always loved her grandmother, even when she had called her names such as 'Old Fogey." Rose knew that Emma was a religious woman, even if she did have a bit of an Irish temper. And Rose felt that if there was anyone she knew who knew God, it had to be Emma. She wanted to understand some things and maybe Emma could help her. Rose was eighteen years old now, and old enough to ask Nick if she could borrow the car, so she did.

Emma had long ago moved into the little granny style home in Goodlettsville. The house was not tiny and it wasn't huge. She had painted it green and put up lattices in the flower bed out front. The house had a comfortable sized front porch with a porch swing. Around the back of the house was a small trailer. Emma had let her grandkids use it as somewhat of an extra bedroom if they wanted to hang out there instead being stuck up in the house when they came over to visit, even though the interior of the house was cozy. She had decorated the kitchen with pictures of people praying, and a plaque of the Lord's prayer. Her wallpaper was floral, and the smell of her chicory nut coffee was absolutely titillating. Rose had arrived mid-morning for her first visit with her grandma in a very long time.

Clarence had died years earlier.

Following the smell of the chicory coffee, Rose found Emma in the den area with her cup of coffee and her Bible in her lap. Rose was instantly sorry for all of the grief that had existed between her and Emma and between Emma and Margie. They were family, and yet they had fought for each other and against each other. It just didn't make any sense to Rose.

She gave her grandmother a hug and a kiss on the cheek. Her skin was so soft. Rose had a flash of when she was very young and she and her siblings had gone with Emma to visit her family's old homestead in Hickman County. She remembered the creek running in front of the yard—how cool and refreshing it had been to play there. She was overwhelmed by nostalgia and wished she was still a little girl that could sit on her Grandmommie's lap. Rose sat on the couch next to the big easy chair where Emma was sitting.

"So, tell me, child. What brings you all the way out here to see your old granny? I haven't seen you in...ages, it seems like."

Rose was not sure where to begin. "Grandmommie, I need some help, help to understand some things."

"Okay, Rose. Go on."

"You know that Tosha girl?"

"You mean Tony's girlfriend?"

"Um, yes."

"Yes, I know who you're talking about. So, what about her?"

"I don't know. She's just strange. I mean, really weird. I think she's doing witchcraft in our home."

"Oh now, Rose..."

"Wait, Grandmommie. There's more. I had a dream when we were living in New York. I can still remember it as if it was yesterday. In this dream, our dad was once again in his military uniform. He was going to some kind of meeting. Suddenly, there was this...this spirit that appeared. It was scaring us, and we were crying and saying, 'Daddy, daddy, please don't go.' But, he said, 'Children, I must go, but I'll be back.' He left us there with that spirit. Karen knew some kind of word that could make the spirit disappear, so we gathered around her. Every time the spirit appeared, she would say that word and the spirit would disappear again. But in my dream, I became so frightened and so stressed that I left the house and left Tony, Anna and Karen there. There was a big hill behind our house, and in the dream, I walked to the other side of the hill and I was gone for a year.

When I came back, the spirit had killed my brother and sisters. Grandmommie, I don't know how to say this...that spirit, it was Tosha. I remember the face in the dream. It was her."

Emma listened intently to Rose. "Well, I know that Tosha's father owned a pharmacy. I know that because I got my prescriptions filled there for years. It seems that I remember hearing that Tosha was a cheerleader in school, a very normal kind of girl."

"A cheerleader? How was that possible? She is a witch, Grandmommie. She is no cheerleader, for Pete's sake!"

"I understand, Rose. But, it may be that she was getting drugs from her father's pharmacy. Taking all those drugs would have easily caused her to become changed. It changes everyone." Rose knew her grandmother was right this time, as she knew in her heart that she had definitely changed from the person she once was. "As for the dream you had, God does give people dreams, sometimes to warn us. Look here, I have it taped on the inside of my Bible cover." Rose wondered what she meant by that.

When Emma opened her Bible, there typed out and taped to the inside of the front cover was Numbers 12:6: "And he said, Hear now my words: If there be a prophet among you, I the LORD will make myself known unto him in a vision, and will speak unto him in a dream."

Emma continued, "So, you see, Rose, you have a gift. It is from God. It's a prophetic gift, but you don't know how to use it yet. You're still very young, honey." Emma seemed to hesitate a bit, as if grasping for words. "I have a confession to make, Rose."

What had her grandmother done that she needed to confess to her, Rose, a sinner?

"The Lord gave me a dream once which I failed to heed." Emma sighed and looked as if she would cry. "A week before your mother met your father, I had a dream one night that my middle daughter, your Aunt Lorraine was pregnant. She was sitting on a wooden stool and crying. And in the background there stood a man yelling at her as if he were lecturing her or something. He had dark hair and was dark skinned. The day my cousin Joe brought your dad to our home, deep inside I knew that he was the face I had seen in that dream.

Rose gasped. She couldn't believe what she was hearing. "Now, wait a minute! You saw my dad's face in your dream, where he was married to Aunt Lorraine. He was mean to her, and he showed up, in the flesh, at your home with your cousin Joe. But you allowed mom to marry him anyway, and she was only sixteen? Why, Grandmommie?"

Emma's face reflected her weariness and her age in that moment. "You wouldn't understand, Rose. In those days, women didn't work much outside the home. I had five children to feed. Your own grandpa was a drunk, and he didn't like to work. Then I met Clarence and married him. He was a hard worker. But, one day, your Aunt Lil, when she was just a little thing, came to me crying and told me that Clarence had done something bad to her. I tried to protect my girls from him, and signing for your mom to marry Jose was the only way I could see to get her away from him..."

Rose was astonished. "But, Grandmommie, they were your girls! Couldn't you have just left Clarence?"

"Rose, I knew you wouldn't understand. I had no way to feed my kids other than Clarence. I didn't have a trade skill. All I knew was being a mother and a wife, and as I said, most women could not find a job outside the home in those days." She was crying now. "I feel so bad. I let my poor baby girl Margie walk right into the arms of a monster, but I just didn't know what to do. I know I should have protected her and all my girls better."

And then, Emma confirmed something for Rose that she had long suspected, "But, Rose, there was something dark about your father. I knew it. I knew it because of my dream. I don't know what he was into, whether it was witchcraft or what. Sometimes I found myself wondering if he was a spy. You know he was in the U.S. military, but he often would receive literature in the mail from Russia about Communism. I don't know, sweetie. I will tell you this— in the Old

Testament, the Bible talks about the worship of idols or false gods. The Lord says there that He is a jealous God, punishing children for the sins of their parents, to the third and fourth generation of those who reject Him."

"Rose, I hope this is not a curse that was passed down, is all I can say, honey. You were raised up in the church as a young child. God tells us in the word that if we train a child in the way he should go, when he is old, he will not depart from it. I know you have strayed, but I am believing that when you are older, you will return to the truth. No matter what, just know this, Rose, whatever you go through, whatever happens, I will be praying, honey. And remember, look for the ancient paths, Rose, and where the good way lies, walk in it."

"But, Grandmommie, if you ask me, it sounds like there are plenty of curses to go around in this family. I don't think there was just one." And what in the world did Grandmommie mean by the ancient paths anyway?

CHAPTER 29

How quickly tragedy can strike, we never realize until it comes. When Rose woke up that Friday, it seemed like any other day to her. She could not possibly have known what lay in store for her that day. As has already been stated, every day was a new world for Rose. She never knew what to expect from day to day. As a matter of fact, she had no structure at all in her life that summer. She was living in a house of seven people, and they all seemed to be going in their own direction most of the time. At times, it truly felt like she was in a house of ships passing in the night.

As fate would have it, this day, Nick and Anna were both home at the same time as Rose. Rose had snuck into the back yard and smoked a joint. Since most of the neighborhood was smoking marijuana those days, no one noticed that her cigarette had a different aroma than her regular pack of Marlboros would have had. She finished the joint and went back inside to fold towels. As soon as she began folding the towels, she heard a knock on the front door. She stiffened like a board. Where was Anna? Why wasn't she answering the door? But, Anna wasn't answering the door. Rose reluctantly put down the towels and walked into the living room.

The Ancient Paths

The weather was warm, so the door was open, but the screen door was latched. She saw two men in dark suits standing on her porch. While she was obviously shaken, she tried to look casual, which was darn near impossible for her at that point. Had someone died?

One of the men identified himself and held up his badge. "Agent Fielding with the FBI, Miss. Is Mr. Nicholas Bella here?" Rose was dumfounded—the FBI! She was stoned out of her freaking gourd! She nodded her head and indicated that she would go get her stepfather. She had not been able to say a word yet.

She first found Anna who had been in her room listening to music the whole time. Rose grabbed her by the arm and said, "Come on Anna. We need to go for a walk."

"What for, sissie?"

"Never mind. Just come with me."

Rose and Anna found Nick in his and Margie's bedroom resting. Since being on the nightshift, he could often be found resting during the day. "Nick, there are a couple of guys from the FBI at the door looking for you," Rose whispered. He nodded solemnly and rose to go meet the FBI agents. Rose and Anna followed Nick to the front door, and as soon as he unlocked the front door to allow the men to enter the house, Rose and Anna walked out the front door as the men were walking in. The girls scampered out the door and took off running. They ran until they were both out of breath.

Anna was both fascinated and perplexed when she realized she had been running for ten minutes, and she didn't even know why. "Sissy...what's going on?"

"I don't know, Anna. I am stoned and I don't even know. Let's just walk somewhere, anywhere." Rose had caught her second wind and started to move again, but this time at a slower pace and Anna naturally followed her.

"Who were those guys, sissie?" Anna wanted to know.

"FBI."

"FBI! What did they want with Nick?"

"Well, Anna, if I had to guess, it probably has to do with all that junk he's been lifting from the warehouse where he works. It's kind of hard to get by with stealing an entire living room suit, clocks and expensive silverware."

"I wonder what'll happen to Nick."

"I hope nothing bad. He's a good stepdad and I like him. Remember his nephew who's the politician? Maybe he'll be able to help Nick. Nick's family are full blooded Greeks, and some of them are pretty well connected."

At that very moment, a black Cadillac pulled up to the curb and inside were two questionable looking characters. The man who was driving was a burly, bearded guy who had one eye which looked crossed. The other man in the car actually put Rose in mind of a weasel. His eyes were beady, his hair was long, dark and thinning at the top. The weasel was the first to speak. "Hey, where you girls going? Do you need a ride?"

They were tired and it was so hot. Anna was the trusting soul, so she blurted out, "Sure. We could use a ride. It's pretty hot."

Standing there, looking at these two strange men and looking at the interior of their car, which was entirely black, Rose had a very bad feeling. She did not want to get in that car, and whispering to Anna, she told her so.

"Rose, they're not gonna hurt us. I've met that little skinny guy before."

"I don't care. I don't want to do this." But, she did. It was getting late in the day, it was hot, and she did not want to go back home to see what was going on there. So, against her better judgment and all her instincts, Rose got into the car with her sister and the two men she had never laid eyes on.

Once she was in the backseat inside the car, Rose's apprehension only intensified. She was not only seeing the black interior, she was literally seeing and feeling the presence of darkness throughout the car. When the burly guy with the eye that was crossed turned and looked at her, Rose's heart sank. She began questioning herself. How far had she herself sunk that she would do something like this, getting into a car with two men whom she instinctively knew were not good? She was the older sister and she should have stopped her little sister from getting in the car too. She was not sure of anything at that moment.

Anna and Rose had the promise of lines of cocaine if they wanted to hang out with the two men. Unfortunately, Rose was swayed by her lust for the drug, so she finally relented and agreed to go wherever the men wanted to take them. Whose house they ended up at, Rose was unsure of. She only knew that they were somewhere in a house with the two men. In contrast to Rose, Anna seemed at ease since she had apparently at some point in time met the weasel before.

When the lines of cocaine were set down in front of Rose, she greedily snorted the two fat lines up her nose. And it only took seconds for her to realize that this was not cocaine. Her vision was rapidly failing and everything around her appeared to melt away. In her fear and confusion, she screamed, "What was this stuff? It's not cocaine! What is this?"

The last thing she saw was the terrified look on her sister's face as she heard the weasel say, "PCP." Then everything went dark.

***

What happened after the darkness and before she woke up, Rose did not know. When she did awake, she was in a taxi cab and was being dropped off at the deli where her mother worked. She was not sure how she had gotten in the cab; she didn't know where her sister was; she didn't know much of anything. She didn't even know how she had gotten the money to pay the cab driver. But, she paid him and painstakingly walked into the busy delicatessen during lunch rush hour. Margie took one look at Rose and knew something was horribly wrong. Rose was walking sideways and having difficulty standing. Margie ushered her to a seat.

"Rose, what's wrong? What happened to you?"

Rose looked at her mother, opened her mouth to say something, and tears flowed down her face. She couldn't stop crying and she was unable to formulate the sounds to say anything. Margie told her, "Look, Anna's at home. She's okay. I don't know everything that happened, but I do know you are not okay. I can't leave right now, but

I want you to eat something while you're here, then I'm going to give you cab fare to get home. Okay?" She had no choice but to agree with her mother.

The months that followed were brief snippets of reality combined with something of a living hell consisting of periods of darkness. Rose's contact with the real world was sketchy at best. Most of her time was spent lying in her bed and one by one, family members would stop in to talk to her, to counsel her.

She opened her eyes and Tony was in her room, sitting in a rocking chair, talking to her.

"Sis, how are you? You know, life is difficult at best. Sometimes when I don't know what to say, and I find myself grasping for words, fumbling for the words, and they refuse to come, I just say nothing. You need to pull it together." It seemed so long ago since she had actually seen her brother. And what did he mean by that anyway?

The next time Rose opened her eyes, there was Laurie, talking to her and trying to make her laugh. "Rose, seriously girlfriend, haven't you napped long enough? You need to get up out of that bed and put your face on!" Rose wanted to laugh at her, but try as she may to formulate a coherent response, the only thing that would come out of Rose's mouth was bitter sobs.

The Ancient Paths

One day Rose was roused by Anna. Anna had been with Rose that fateful night of Rose's overdose, and yet, for some reason, Anna had not understood the seriousness of the drug that Rose had ingested that night. Anna had never touched it that evening. PCP, it was nothing more than an animal tranquilizer which had killed several other kids recently. So, Anna had simply thought that Rose had lost it for no real reason. "We all go to the other side of the looking glass sometime, Rose. But, see, there's nothing in there. It's just you." What did that mean? What had happened to her?

The next time Rose opened her eyes, she was standing alone in the kitchen in the darkness. Everyone was asleep. How had she gotten there? She was completely unaware that she had been roaming the house at night for months while others slept. For all practical purposes, she had become like a ghost to her family.

Then one day, there was a breakthrough. It was daytime, and as she lay in her bed, it was almost as though she could hear someone say to her, "Rose, if you don't wake up now, you're never going to see your family again." In that instant, memories came flooding back, and she remembered how much she loved her family and how close they had once been. She felt so far away from them right now, and yet, she had been in her home the whole time. She had crossed that fine line and stepped over to the other side of reality.

Rose pulled herself up out of the bed and for the first time in a very long time, did not feel the urge to turn around and climb right back in. When she walked into the living room, there sat Karen by herself. So Rose started questioning her. "Karen, what happened?"

"You lost it, Rose. Everyone knew you had lost it, but they just didn't know why. We were all worried you would never come back. But, I guess because of Mom's intelligence and her and Grandmommie's faith, she knew you would come back. The doctors wanted to put you somewhere, but Mom wanted to keep you here at home. It's like you were gone and there was a spirit here in your place."

Rose could see the anguish reflected in sister's face. "What kind of spirit, Karen?"

"A spirit of sadness. Mom kept saying she wanted her child back."

"What about Nick? What happened to him?"

"Nothing. He was able to get off with a slap on the wrist."

Then she asked the question "Karen, how long have I been like this?"

Karen could barely maintain her composure. "A year."

"Oh my God, a whole year?" Rose thought she would lose it again. A whole year! She sank to her knees and laid her head in Karen's lap. Her little sister stroked her hair as the realization slowly dawned on Rose that she was now in a time warp. She had lost one year of her life, and for what? For madness?

"What about Tosha? Is she still living here?

"No, she moved out a long time ago. She drops by to visit from time to time." At that very moment, as if on cue, there was a knock at the door and Tosha strolled in. She had gained weight, but she still managed to dress in the most bizarre manner possible. She had on her grey robe with her brown lace up boots once again.

Rose slowly stood up and walked to where Tosha was standing, coming face to face with Tosha to confront her, once and for all. "Tosha, exactly who are you?"

"Me? I'm coo-coo. You're coo-coo too."

"I'm not coo-coo. But I know who you are now. You're that spirit I saw in my dream as a child, aren't you? Only you weren't just a spirit, you were flesh and blood. You can't be here anymore. So, it's time for you to be gone."

Tosha laughed mockingly at Rose, "No one will ever believe you.

Everyone will say you're crazy. I've still got your family, Rose. Just look at them. They are mine." And with that, Tosha turned and left, never saying why she had stopped by in the first place. What did she mean that she still had Rose's family?

Rose stole a glance at Karen. She was dressed identical to the way Tosha often dressed, in the rolled up blue jeans, bells attached to her belt loops, boots and scarf. Before it had just been Anna who had fallen into that pattern of dress. Something definitely had happened here in the last year. Rose was certain of that. But she was back now. She had gone to the other side, just like in her dream, and that spirit had tried to claim her family.

The following morning, for the first time in a year, Rose meandered out of her room at six a.m. in her pajamas with her hair in disarray and rubbing her eyes. She was up early enough to join her mother and stepfather for breakfast before they left for work. Over the morning paper, they sat at the dining room table having coffee, bacon and eggs. Bacon! It was Rose's favorite meat of all time. What a warm and familiar feeling it was to see her parents in the morning again. It was as though for the first time she was seeing the true value in the small things she had taken for granted such as seeing her mom and stepdad doing something as normal as having their coffee, breakfast while reading the morning paper. Where had her mind been for the past year?

"Margie, look what the dogs drug in," Nick chuckled. He was glad to see that Rose was finally coming back to herself. He turned off the laughter rather quickly and changed his tone. "I'm glad you're up, Rose. Me and your mom thought you might need to see this." Without any further explanation, he gently laid the morning newspaper on the table for Rose to see the headlines on the page. She picked up the paper, moving her lips as she read. She had often dreamed about this, and had even longed for it, but now that it had actually happened, she was numb. Or perhaps it was just too much too soon for her.

The morning headlines read, "THREE KILLED IN CAR CRASH." Tosha's name was listed as one of the three young people involved in the fatal wreck. Rose couldn't get past Tosha's name. This was not computing. "What? What is this? She was just here yesterday. What happened?" She looked to both her parents for answers. They knew that there had been bad blood between Rose and Tosha, and perhaps their eyes had been blinded to the depth of the bad feelings between the two girls, but they knew this news was going to have a profound effect on their daughter either way.

It was Margie who spoke up "Well, honey, it seems that Tosha had apparently moved to New Orleans sometime within this past year. The irony if it was this--she had recently returned to Nashville to attend the funeral of one of her high school friends who had been killed in a motorcycle accident. I think you met him before, that nice looking boy Barry with long brown hair who took you for a ride on his motorcycle."

Rose buried her face in her hands. She knew exactly who her mother was referring to. Tosha had repeatedly asked Rose to meet her friend whom she had described as a cosmic cowboy and go out with him on his motorcycle. At Tosha's persistence that Rose meet Barry, Rose had finally acquiesced. It had been a one-time date only. Speechless, she looked at her mother and nodded.

Margie continued with the story of what had happened to Tosha. "The trio had been on their back way to New Orleans. One of the people in the car was Tosha's roommate from New Orleans. The third person in the car was one of Tosha's Nashville friends named Doug who had agreed to drive them back home to New Orleans. Tosha's mother and sister were in a car following them when the wreck occurred. And...there's one other thing, Rose."

Rose's first thought was, "What else is there? They're dead, so what else could there possibly be?" She looked at her mother through eyes that were struggling to grasp what all had gone on within the past twenty-four hours. Rose still felt like she was in a bit of a fog, and the impact of the story came barreling down upon her full force. Her head was reeling. What just happened? She could barely gather her thoughts. Tosha must have stopped by yesterday before leaving town to head back to New Orleans. If Rose had thought that the removal of her antagonist would make her life easier, she didn't feel quite so sure now. "What, Mom? What else?"

Margie drew in a deep breath and slowly exhaled. "They were all thrown from the car, Rose. All three of them had broken necks."

"Oh my God," Rose sighed. Hadn't she once said that she wished Tosha would just die? "What have I done?"

Part 3

CHAPTER 30

At the age of twenty-eight, Rose had been married, divorced and had moved back home with her parents. Since the days when Tosha had lived in their home as teenagers, she had not seen much of her siblings. Anna was in California, Karen had moved out before she ever turned eighteen, and Tony had moved to the outskirts of town.

Rose had struggled with what to do for a profession. She had dropped out of college after only one semester. She had worked at numerous office jobs only to end up burned out and struggling with the fact that she was tied down to a chair and desk every day; therefore, she had fluctuated between office work and waitress work. And at this point in her life, Rose found herself working at the Eagle's Nest Restaurant and Listening Room, in an upper class neighborhood where she waited tables, and many of her customers were often the rich and famous of Nashville.

The bar was a small one but quite popular with the locals. Several country music acts who had debuted there had gone on to find national acclaim and recognition. The stage was in the front of the room, the antique wooden bar was in the back, and small round tables filled the space in between. It was a small place. Around the corner and beyond the bar were the men's and women's restrooms.

Smoke filled the room as everyone lit up cigarettes during the band's break. As Rose stood at the end of the bar with her tray, waiting for the next customer to come in and sit at one of her tables, she observed groups of women who were coming out of the restroom together. Two women in particular had caught Rose's attention when they came out of the ladies' room and were sniffing and rubbing their noses. Both had eyes that looked like roadmaps. It didn't take a rocket scientist to figure out what they had been doing in the bathroom. Down at the other end of the bar was a man who had obviously had too much to drink, either that or something else. His head was laid down on the bar, and he appeared to be unconscious. To her surprise, Rose was jealous that these people had come in for their entertainment, and as messed up as they were, she was here to serve them. And at the same time, she was beginning to wonder if she possibly didn't belong there at all.

As busy as the place was, no one else came in and sat at Rose's tables for the rest of the night after eight o'clock; and of all the people in the bar, no one talked to Rose, not even to say hello. When she repeatedly approached the tables where she already had customers seated, no one wanted anything else to drink after their first cocktail. She didn't quite know what it was, but there was something a little different about this night. Was it her imagination or had she actually seen what appeared to be a white barrier, almost like a shield which separated her from the other people in the bar that night? It was as though there was something which kept others from communicating with her or approaching her. It was like she was being separated. She felt almost alien in her surroundings.

Rose had had enough, so she asked permission to leave work early that night. "Larry, my tables aren't doing anything. No one is buying more drinks and it's already getting late. Is it okay if I knock off early?"

The bartender, Larry who was also the manager, agreed. "Sure. It does look like you've been kind of slow tonight for some reason, and it's been busy here." But she was not ready to go home yet, so once she had left work, Rose headed down to After Hours, the local hotel with a bar that was open until six a.m. every morning. It was one of the few places in town where people could still congregate to hang out after the night clubs had closed.

The place was dimly lit as Rose walked in like a stranger seeking refuge from a storm. Small clusters of people sitting on couches in the main room mingled over drinks. Rose headed over to the bar, "A glass of Merlot, please." She got lucky and found a spot on one of the couches. She once again found herself feeling somewhat alienated. She sat down beside a man and woman whom she recognized and had met on numerous occasions. But they were local musicians who were too caught up in their own egos to notice her.

The Ancient Paths

And then she saw him. Rose had not seen him in ages, about eleven years ago, to be precise. She easily recognized Roland whom she had once met at in the kitchen the night of the big party at the mansion when she and Laurie had stripped down and gone skinny dipping in the pool. She looked over at Roland and waved. He flashed a full smile of beautiful white teeth against a dark tan. His hair had grown out some, and his brown hair streaked with blond from the sun against his tan made him even more handsome. He had also grown a beard. His eyes were big, bright, and blue, which had seemed odd to Rose. There was something quite natural, even wild about his look, but it had a very strong appeal to Rose. She had once heard someone describe him as "just a beautiful person." He was indeed.

Roland scooted in between Rose and the person on her left and sat down beside her. "Can I buy you a glass of wine?" he offered.

"Thanks, but I already had one, Roland. Have you got any recreational drugs, perhaps?" Rose had not wasted any time getting down to business.

"Um, yes, I do," he smiled, "but not with me. I have some MDA at home. Have you ever tried that?"

"Oh boy, yeah, I have, a long time ago. I don't really care to do psychedelics anymore. I've had some bad experiences with that stuff."

"Well, this stuff is pure, I promise."

How could she not trust this handsome guy? He was gorgeous and...organic was the only word she could think of to describe it to herself.

"Okay, so are we going to your place then?"

"Yes, if we want to get high we are. I can drive you there if you want. It's in Bordeaux and out in the country. It's up to you."

She wasn't wild about leaving her car parked at the hotel, but she would. "Okay, I'll leave my car here and get it later."

***

On the way to Roland's home, the atmosphere seemed to change. It became electric. It started raining and lightning, and as they came closer to the remote area where Roland lived, they came to a screeching halt where a tree had fallen, blocking the road. "What's going on?" Rose nervously asked.

"Don't worry, I know another road we can take. It will be alright," Roland assured her.

Rose began inhaling deep breaths and trying to quell her rising level of anxiety. She just wanted to get off the road at this point. "We can do this," she kept whispering under her breath. "We can do this." Perhaps it was merely the inclement weather which had set in on them, but she felt a sense of urgency that they reach their destination as soon as possible.

Which route Roland took that eventually led them to his home, Rose had no clue. There were too many dark, winding roads in this part of the county. She had never been to this area, at least not that she could recall. But finally, Roland pulled into a gravel driveway at a small, charming cottage looking home. "This is it. It's not much, but it's home."

Rose was not sure what she had expected, but this place reminded her of a quaint little grandmother home from a fairytale she may have read as a child.

"I'll run ahead and unlock the door so that you don't have to stand out in the rain getting wet," Roland offered.

"Sounds good to me. I'll be right behind you." She made a mad dash to the side door where Roland had entered the house and stood waiting for her. "Well, I got a little wet, but not too bad."

"I'm sure I have a dry shirt I can let you try on, and we can put your blouse in the dryer, if you like."

Rose's instinct was to think, "Ah, I don't know. This is definitely going to lead to something, and I don't know that I want to go there." But, her top was soaked, and she was feeling a bit of a chill in the air. "Okay, please, that would be great. Thank you."

While Roland browsed through his closet and drawers for something that Rose could change into, she checked out the little house. It was incredibly clean and cozy for a guy's home. The couch was in the middle of the living room and there was a fireplace to the right of the room. A fire would be inviting right about now. The kitchen definitely felt country with its white cabinets and brightly painted yellow walls. Roland obviously had a creative touch. It had been a long time since Rose had been anywhere beyond the inner city limits of Nashville, and it felt, well, it felt good.

"Here you go. The bathroom is down the hallway to the left, so you can change in there if you like. I'll throw your top in the dryer."

After Roland had tossed Rose's blouse in the dryer, he joined her in the living room. He selected some Jackson Browne music for ambiance, started a fire in the fireplace then sat on the couch with Rose. They sat looking at one another, neither knowing exactly what to say or do next. But then Roland reached into his pocket and extracted a piece of tightly wrapped aluminum foil. He unwrapped it, laid out some lines of white powder on the coffee table, rolled up a dollar bill, then snorted two of the lines up his nose and handed the rolled up dollar bill to Rose. She inhaled the other two lines up her nostrils then immediately started rubbing her nose.

"This stuff's a little different. What did you say it was?"

"It's MDA with some added cocaine mixed in it."

"That's right! Crap, I forgot! I haven't done MDA or any psychedelics in ages. I hate that stuff."

Roland reached over and placed his hand on top of hers for reassurance. "It'll be okay. I promise." With his hand still holding hers, Roland lifted Rose's hand to examine it more closely. "Nice ring." On Rose's hand was the ring Jose had given her on his deathbed. It was a sparkling purple stone. She had never worn it until the last few years.

"My father gave it to me."

"Is it an A…?"

"Yeah, it's an Alexandrite. The colors have been amazing to watch when they change."

"Can I see it for a moment? They are actually rather rare."

The Ancient Paths

Rose held out her hand for Roland, and he tried to pull the ring off her finger, only it wouldn't come off. Rose motioned for him to stop.

"It's been stuck on there ever since I first put it on."

That caught his attention. "And how long has that been?"

"Two years."

"Rose, now listen to me. Besides being a videographer, I am also a jeweler. Wait, I have something I want to show you." He walked out of the room and came back with a beautiful brass necklace with numerous fringes which were laden with turquoise. He explained the design of the necklace to her. "Each strand is exactly one millimeter shorter than the next one." The symmetry of the design was incredible.

"Beautiful," was all she could say. It *was* beautiful.

Roland reached over the top of Rose's head and fastened the necklace on her. "Listen to me, Rose. That ring...it needs to come off. And the main reason is this--if by chance some freak accident occurred and you should get stung by a bee or bitten by a snake, your finger could swell so badly that the ring would cut off your circulation."

"But how? How will I get it off?"

"Let me cut it off?"

Rose jumped up off the couch at that. Her anxiety level had just accelerated by about a hundred points. "But what if you miss, and get my finger instead?"

"That necklace you're wearing—I made that. Remember? One has to have very steady hands and be able to work with fine details in order to get the pieces to be exactly one millimeter shorter than the one next to it. I can do this, Rose. How about if I rub your hand, saturate it with lotion first? I think I can loosen it that way and just slip it off your hand."

"I've tried that before, but okay." Rose nodded her consent.

Roland left the room and returned with a large bottle of lotion. He covered her hand in the lotion, set the bottle on the coffee table, then he slowly massaged the lotion into her hand. Finally, he began tugging at the ring and was able to move the ring further up on her finger. "It's coming. I can feel it," he said. And just as he thought he was about to have the ring in position to slide it over her knuckle and off her finger, suddenly, it visibly tightened.

Rose was whimpering, "Please stop. It's getting tighter."

"Just another minute and I'll have it, Rose."

The Ancient Paths

The ring tightened again and Rose's finger turned purple as veins bulged from the tightness of the ring.

"My ears are ringing, Roland. Please stop." And it was hurting, badly.

"It's fighting us, Rose. I saw that ring tighten its grip on you. This is not my imagination either."

Tears streamed down her face. "I know it. This may sound ridiculous at a time like this, but I have a crazy question for you, Roland. Do you believe in God? Not *just* a god, not just *any* god, but do you believe in God?" For some reason, she felt that before she could go any further, she had to know right then, at that moment, what his answer was.

In spite of the dilemma of the ring, Roland tried to gauge his response and give a thoughtful answer. "In spite of what it looks like, I do believe in God, Rose. I believe in being good...because it is good to be good. I am fairly sensitive to spiritual matters, I suppose, even though I obviously still have a lot of maturing to do. My grandmother was born in Puerto Rico when it had been called Puerto Spain, long ago. She had been heiress to a large amount of real estate. She was sent to a convent, but later when she fell in love and married, she was disinherited. She then came to America, but she made sure we all knew about the God of heaven and earth. I guess I've just never learned to walk the straight and narrow path, Rose, but I believe."

Wow. She had never heard such an intriguing story. Rose was not sure of her own reasoning ability just then, since she was tripping her butt off on MDA and cocaine, but she knew she must press forward. "I don't care what you have to do, please just get this ring off of my finger."

"My pliers are in my toolbox in the shed. It will only take a minute to get them."

"But you can't leave me in here by myself," she reasoned, now in full panic mode.

"Watch me out the window," he told her.

She eagerly nodded. Roland headed toward the kitchen door, which was the same entrance Rose had passed through when she first arrived. It was now early dawn, so Rose was able to clearly see Roland as he made the short trip to the garage and then ducked inside it. She held her breath until a moment later when he came back out of the garage carrying his toolbox. She now felt an invisible cord had bound her to this man for that moment in time. How many years had it been since she had met him at T.J.'s that night so long ago? Ten or more?

Rose opened the kitchen door for Roland. She kept reminding

271

herself that she was high on psychedelics and this may not even be real, but somehow she believed it was. They were not just tripping on MDA, they had embarked on a journey together. Rummaging through his toolbox, Roland found his pliers and held them up for Rose's inspection and approval. They were needle nose pliers, much slimmer than what Rose had envisioned, so she felt a burst of confidence when she saw them.

"Yes, quick. Do it now," Rose told him before she could lose her nerve.

Roland took Rose's hand and firmly held the ring with his fingers. As he positioned the pliers against the ring, suddenly, out of the quiet of the still country morning and the presence of the knowledge that this was their journey together, bolts of lightning and rays of purple, brown, aqua green, the colors of the Alexandrite burst forth from the ring and filled the air in the room.

Rose closed her eyes and looked away, screaming and sobbing hysterically. Roland on the other hand was too mesmerized by the sight; therefore, he was momentarily blinded by the colors and stumbled backward onto the floor, hitting his head, rendering him semiconscious. There in their midst, looming over Rose was an apparition of Tosha, easily three feet off the ground.

"So you thought you could escape me. But, guess what Sweetie, I've come back, back to take you home with me. Now tell your boyfriend goodbye. It's time to go." And just like that, she reached down and grabbed Rose's right arm and pulled, trying to drag her into the pits of hell with her. Rose's feet were coming up off the ground and Rose could feel herself slipping from this dimension into the realm of the unknown.

Rose found her voice and screamed with all her might, "Roland! Help me, please!"

Roland had been dazed but not completely knocked out. Upon hearing Rose's piercing cry for help, he regained his wits, and letting loose a yell that shook the room, "No!!!" he jumped up and charging like a bull, he grabbed Rose's left hand, loosing her from the grip of the apparition. Holding onto her for dear life as Tosha tried to regain her grip on Rose and pull her toward the dark pit of infinity, he placed the pliers against the ring. He uttered a quick prayer under his breath, "God help me." He felt such a surge of power in his hands at that moment, and closing his eyes, he snapped the pliers and he could hear the ring snap too.

Rose fell unconscious to the ground as the apparition slowly evaporated, emitting blood curdling screams and reaching toward Rose as it went, "I came back for her soul, and it's mine. Do you hear me? It's mine!"

Roland shook his head in disbelief and chuckled to himself, "Man, what a great first date. I can hardly wait for the encore." He knew for a fact that Rose had been set free of something, whatever it was, that night. But somehow, he felt like there was more.

CHAPTER 31

After the "ring trip" as Rose and Roland had dubbed it, Rose's world did not exactly become perfect overnight, but things certainly began to change. Things changed because all of a sudden nothing was happening in her life now. The drama and excitement of her teenager years had passed long ago. She was at the point in her life when she knew it was time to grow up and be a responsible adult; yet, everything was now at a standstill for her. Her car had quit running, she had no money to get it fixed, her parents had no money to loan her; therefore, she had no way of getting around, so she was no longer working. Since she was living with her parents once again, and they had moved to the edge of the west side of town, just far enough away that even the city bus did not go there, she was in essence, stuck.

In addition to her sister Anna being in California, Laurie too had long ago moved there, and Rose was feeling the need to call her and hear her voice. She missed her best friend so. It felt like everyone that she had once known and been close to was now gone. She couldn't shake the feeling that she was now alone. When she had been a child, Rose had always looked forward to the day when she could be an adult and be her own boss, only she had not done such a good job of that either.

When Laurie answered the phone that night, Rose couldn't wait to share with her all of the recent events of her life, including the incident with the ring. Laurie was a voice of reason from far away now. "Rose, remember Jeff from high school? Well, I heard that he's become a born again Christian. I heard that one night when he was playing in a nightclub a stranger, someone he'd never met before, came to the club and talked to him, telling him that he was going to serve the Lord and play his music for the Lord. Remember, he had never even met the man before. And now Jeff's playing guitar at a church. So, it turned out that the stranger was right. I heard that Jeff said the man must have been an angel. You should call him, Rose."

In the years following high school, Rose had actually run into Jeff when she had been out and about at places like the grocery store. She had been aware from the time she had met him during high school days that he had a compassion and understanding unlike most people she had known. He was the sensitive type.

"I knew that he had become a born again Christian, Laurie, but I found it difficult to talk to him whenever I would run into him. I'm not even really sure what born again means. I just wasn't sure how to take him because he's so different now."

"Give it a try, Rose. Call him. Go see him. What have you got to lose?"

The Ancient Paths

On Friday evening, as much as Rose hated to, she approached her parents to ask if she could borrow their car. She felt like such a child now. "Where are you going, Rose?" Margie wanted to know.

"Don't worry, mom. I promise, I'm not going out to drink. I just want to go visit an old friend of mine and Tony's from high school."

For years and years, Jeff had played in a rock band as lead guitarist and singer. As far back as high school his band had played at the school and community center dances. After high school, his band had played out west in Vegas, Reno and Tahoe for three years before he returned to Nashville and started playing in nightclubs in the Nashville and Kentucky area. Unknown to Jeff at the time, his mother had been praying for him for years. Other people in her church had been praying for him too.

The few times Rose had run into Jeff in the last year or so she had seen a difference in him, and she had heard the difference in his voice. She had even thought him a bit fanatical, but now here she was, going to visit him because she felt as if he could supply her with some much needed answers which she was so desperately seeking.

Rose knocked on the door, and when Jeff opened it, she was suddenly reminded of how beautiful his eyes were. His eyes had always reminded her of the ocean. They were that perfect blend of blue and green. And yet, she was surprised to realize just how bright and clear Jeff's eyes were. "Were they that clear before?" she wondered. His eyes absolutely sparkled like jewels now.

"Come on in, Rose. What have you been up to?"

She followed Jeff into his living room and sat on the couch across from him in his easy chair. He looked at her and smiled, waiting for an explanation of her visit.

Rose wasn't really sure how to begin. She took a deep breath and dove in. "Jeff, there have just been a long series of things. It's hard to explain." She could not hold back the pain a moment longer. A tear found its way down her cheek. She was mad at herself. She had not meant to lose her composure so quickly and so easily. "What is wrong with me? I need to pull it together," she chastised herself.

Jeff walked out of the room, returning with a couple of Kleenex which he handed to Rose. She dabbed at her eyes. "It's okay, Rose. Just take your time."

"Well, it's like nothing goes right for me. No matter how hard I try, everything I touch is a failure. For example: I've been working at the Eagle's Nest waiting tables. I had a flat tire one night when I got off of work, so I got a ride home from my manager. The next day, I got a ride back to work during the daytime, and I changed the tire myself. I was so proud of myself for doing it and not having to ask someone to do it for me. Well, would you believe after I had changed the tire, put the flat in the trunk and closed the trunk door, I had locked the keys in the trunk? So, I ended up having to pay eighty dollars to have a locksmith come and unlock the trunk for me. I didn't really accomplish much by changing my own tire, did I? Then soon after that, my car just quit working altogether. Now, I'm stuck at home with my parents. Jeff, I feel like I'm cursed. My whole life, I've been chased by bad luck it seems. And recently, I had an experience which is hard to describe. I had a ring that had apparently been cursed, and I had to have it cut off my finger. You want to know the irony of the whole thing?"

"Sure, Rose. What was the irony?

"The irony was this—my father gave me that ring." She then told Jeff in detail the story of the "ring trip."

As she looked deeper into Jeff's eyes, she realized there was a peace there which she had never really seen before and there was a glow about his countenance; a presence of light surrounded him. There was just something she couldn't quite put her finger on, but it was something definitely different. Jeff had not said much up to this point; he had been listening attentively to Rose's story and speaking only when spoken to.

"Rose, it's kind of like this; if you sit in a room without light, it's dark, right?" He reached over and turned off his lamp and darkened the room for emphasis. "And when you turn on the light, the room is filled with that light, enabling you to see. The same is true for our lives. If we walk in spiritual darkness, we see nothing. It's like we're blinded. Once we have the light of God in our lives, we can both see and feel the light. You have been living in the dark, Rose. Think about it, even when you worked, when you got off, it was dark. You were up until sunrise, and then you slept during the daytime. When you got up, guess what? It was dark again. You have literally been living in the darkness, but God is opening your eyes, and you are beginning to see." It was so clear the way he explained it.

In the back of her mind, Rose supposed she had always known there was the one and only true God, but she had never possessed a very large amount of faith, at least not in her opinion, and she had never heard anything about the light before. But that night, looking at Jeff, she realized that God really could change a person. This was definitely not the same Jeff who had once sat in her brother's room with a group of other high school boys getting high. She prayed silently that there was still hope for her.

"Rose, there have been many nights when I have woken up in the middle of the night and thought of you, and I would just start praying." On the heels of the "ring trip," this was a lot for Rose to absorb--so many things happening so fast. "Why don't you visit church with me sometime, Rose? The door's always open there."

And she did, she began attending church regularly with Jeff. Even though Rose had been raised in the church as a child, she had only gone sporadically after her childhood. The truth was that she was afraid the roof would cave in when she walked through the door.

The church Jeff attended was a very small wooden building painted white and it was located in a poor section of town. On a good Sunday there might be fifteen, possibly twenty people in attendance. And yet, Rose had known from the moment she stepped foot into the place that there was something truly spiritual about it; there was a feeling that she had never experienced anywhere else in her life. The presence she felt there was real; it was palpable.

Jeff played guitar with the worship team; he was lead guitarist, just like he had always been only now he was not in a nightclub. Perhaps it was because she was getting the drugs out of her system and could discern the sound better now; maybe it was because he was no longer doing drugs and he actually played better. Whatever the reason, she had never realized what a great guitar player Jeff actually was. As small as the building was, the music literally filled every corner of the room, was very soulful and infiltrated every fiber of her being. It would have been extremely difficult not to be moved by the music.

And yet, even though she was attending church, her financial and professional situation remained in disarray, and Jeff felt burdened for Rose. "I wish I had some clarity about what God is wanting for your life, Rose; I don't though. But I will tell you this. There is a woman at church named Deborah. She has the gift of prophecy, and many times God has revealed things to her about someone who was in desperate need of the Lord in their life. It isn't necessarily always people who haven't found the Lord yet; sometimes it may just be someone who is having a lot of confusion or unhappiness in their life. I'll do this. I'll ask her if there is anything the Lord has revealed to her about your life that she can share with you."

That part of his sentence, "...the gift of prophecy..." echoed in Rose's brain. She had heard that somewhere else only recently, hadn't she? Rose did not know which lady at church Deborah was, but she felt certain she must have seen her at some point since the number of those in attendance was generally rather small. Rose didn't dare to hope that someone might finally be able to help her gain more insight into why her life had been so completely miserable; however, the next time she spoke with Jeff by phone, she brought it up. "Were you ever able to talk to Deborah?" she asked.

"Yeah, I did talk to her, Rose. She said that the Lord had in fact revealed some things to her about you. She wouldn't tell me anything though and she wouldn't let me tell her anything. Said she wants to speak to you personally because she wanted you to know that I had not told her anything. She wants you to know that the things she is going to tell you are straight from God. I'll give you her number and you can even call her tonight." Rose could hear her pulse beating, it got loud.

That evening, Rose paced the floor until it was finally time to call Deborah. She had determined that eight o'clock would be an appropriate time to call her; it would give Deborah enough time to have dinner with her husband and to relax before hearing from Rose. The palms of Rose's hands were clammy as she dialed Deborah's phone number.

It was Deborah who picked up the phone and whose voice Rose heard. "Hello, Deborah. This is Rose. Jeff gave your number to me and told me you had some things you wanted to share with me. Is that right?"

"Yes, honey. That's right. The first time I saw you at church, my heart ached for you. I didn't know if I had ever felt that someone had gone through so much as I knew you had. I began to pray for you. I know that it seems like every time you try to do something, you run into a brick wall and you can't move one way or the other. You have been hurt by so many people in your life that you feel you can trust no one. You have been hurt by many that were supposed to protect you and love you. And sometimes you have felt so hopeless that you have even thought of taking your own life."

Big tears welled up in Rose's eyes and slid down her face. Everything that Deborah had said was, of course, true. Deborah

283

continued, "You have thought of taking your own life even recently, haven't you?" It was true. Just the day before, Rose had contemplated killing herself. But every time she had those thoughts, she would think about the consequences it would have on her soul. She had done many wrong things in her life, but killing herself was something she could not bring herself to do no matter how much she had wanted to do it.

"Honey, the Lord just wants you to know that he loves you. And he knows about all the pain and hurt you've had to go through. You have had much evil come against you all your life, and many times you did not understand what was happening. The Lord is going to begin to bring about a change in your life. But it is not going to be easy for you." Rose could feel such genuine love and concern in Deborah's voice that she couldn't stop crying. She had never heard such compassion in a virtual stranger's voice before.

In spite of reading the Bible, attending church Sunday morning, Sunday evening and Tuesday evening every week, Rose started having hellacious nightmares, and each one brought its own torment for her. It seemed that the harder she tried to get it right, the harder she was fought.

In the first dream, Rose was standing in the kitchen of her parents' home looking out the window, and it was dark outside. She saw a little girl between the ages of eight and ten. She was walking into the woods that were on the hill behind the house. There was an evil presence that appeared to be drawing her into the woods. In the dream, Rose turned and commented to her stepfather who was standing in the kitchen with her, "Look at that little girl. Why is she going into the woods?"

He responded, "The little girl always goes there about this same time every day." In the dream, Rose looked at the clock and it was four o'clock in the morning. The dream was intense enough to wake Rose up, and it had her nerves rattled. As she sat up in bed, staring blankly ahead, it dawned on her. That little girl was her. It was Rose. Why was she walking into the darkness of the woods? What darkness was it that was calling her there, and why was she having that stupid dream?

The nightmare had been so dark that the next evening, Rose was afraid to go to sleep. She began to pray for a peaceful night's sleep. "God, please, please help me to sleep. I'm tired, and I want to sleep without being afraid."

But, it was not to be. When she finally did drift off to sleep, the nightmares came again. This time there was a beautiful castle made out of red stone with a front yard about an acre in size, and the grass was bright green. It almost looked like springtime. The sky was a clear, bright blue, and there were beautiful white birds flying around the rooftops of the castle. The birds were graceful, elegant, mesmerizing to watch. As Rose stood in the front yard of the castle beholding the scene which was so pleasing to the human eye, the birds began to swoop down and attack her. Only, when they dove at her, they bounced off her body. It was as though an invisible shield were protecting her from the attack. Her body stiffened and jerked from the impact of the birds, even though they had actually done her no physical harm. When she woke up, her body was still in spasms.

The next day, Rose called Deborah. "I'm exhausted, Deborah. I haven't been able to sleep because I keep having these insane nightmares that always wake me up, then I'm afraid to go back to sleep. I know my mother thinks I'm losing it. My nerves are shot. But I just can't explain to her what's happening to me. She wouldn't understand. I'm not even sure that I understand anymore."

"Honey, don't you worry. You go to sleep tonight, and just know that I will be praying, and I will call Jeff's mom to pray for you too." Rose remembered what Laurie had said about Jeff's mom praying for him for years. She knew that his mom's prayers were powerful. For the first time in days, Rose was allowed to have a peaceful night's sleep that night.

The following night, the nightmares returned. This time, Rose was looking into a flaming inferno, almost as if she had tunnel vision. All she could see were flames of fire lapping at her from inside a long, deep pit. As she looked into this tunnel of fires, a demon which was flaming red and itself made of fire, jumped out of the flames with his arms reaching straight up as if he were reaching for Rose with the intent of pulling her into the flaming pit. As he reached for her, the fiery figure roared with a sound that was so loud it woke her up. This nightmare had been the daddy of them all. She knew the enemy of her soul aimed to torment her for sure.

Financially, spiritually, morally and emotionally broken, Rose was like a lost soul wandering aimlessly in search of an answer. What could stop this madness? Right now though, she just needed to get some focus and get her head straight. Maybe a good workout would help. Margie had taken the day off work, so she happened to be there. "Mom, will you please give me a ride to the gym today? I'm sorry to always have to bum rides, but I really, really need to go work out. Would you mind?"

It was obvious that her daughter was having difficulty getting her life on track. She knew that Rose had been going to church, but Rose's state of mind was a source of concern for Margie. Maybe the gym would be a good outlet for her. "Sure, honey. I'll give you a ride. Just call me when you're ready to come home."

"Thank you, mom. You're the best."

Rose had gone to the same gym for years after her drug overdose years earlier. She had found that the release of endorphins from exercising helped her to relax and had helped her sense of confidence, until now. At the present, she did not feel confident in the least.

The Ancient Paths

Because she had gone to the same exercise facility for so long, she knew all the employees, the owner, most of the patrons, and she even knew the young girl named Jeanine who babysat in the nursery there.

After Rose had completed her workout, she meandered into the nursery to talk to Jeanine. She didn't feel ready to go home yet. What was there to do at home anyway? It was a quiet day at the gym and she hadn't seen anyone that she recognized in the workout area. Everyone must have had an early morning workout and gone on to other things.

Jeanine was twenty-one years of age. She had long honey blond hair and blue eyes, was a quiet young lady and seemed mature beyond her years. It had always been easy to talk to her. "How was your workout? I really need to work on my thighs." Jeanine was good at making small talk.

"Just fine. I'm trying to get in shape again. It's been awhile since I've been in here," Rose responded.

That was all she had time to get out of her mouth before both her and Jeanine's eyes followed the sight they had caught a glimpse of in their line of peripheral vision. Standing on the other side of the folding wooden gate which separated the nursery from the exercise floor was a little girl who could not have been any older than four or five. But this was no ordinary little girl. There was definitely something noticeably different about her. Her eyes were a deep, dark brown and there was an almost blank expression in those big eyes. It was as though she did not see what was in front of her. Her brown stringy hair hung about her shoulders and she wore bangs. The really peculiar thing about the child was that her hair seemed to be standing straight out from her head, as if all her hair were full of static. The child's presence produced a chilling effect on the two women. Rose was literally shivering.

The little girl looked directly at Rose and stared at her for a moment or two before opening her to mouth to talk to Rose. "Hi. What's your name?" Rose was still transfixed by the child, so much so that she couldn't speak. "Do you want me to give you my phone number so that you can call me and we can talk?" the little girl asked Rose. Still, Rose could only stare at the child. It was not nighttime, and this was not taking place in her sleep. It was broad daylight, she was wide awake, and somehow this possessed child had come to Rose as a living, breathing nightmare. Rose felt fear such as she had never known, and was afraid that her mind had had all it could take, as though she would snap if something didn't happen, and quick.

The little girl had engaged in a stare down with Rose, and suddenly, the little girl's mother appeared, took the little girl by the hand and led her out the front door of the gym. Rose and Jeanine stood, staring for a moment even after the mother and child had left the gym.

Neither woman knew what to say after the encounter. She looked at Jeanine to see what her response would be to the scene they had just witnessed. It was obvious that Jeanine too was visibly shaken. Finally, Rose broke the ice. "I had cold chills go up and down my arms and my back when she was standing there. I have never in my life seen a child with that kind of appearance. She almost didn't even look like a child."

"That was the devil in that child," Jeanine slowly responded.

That confirmed it for Rose. Jeanine *had* seen the whole thing too! But, how on earth did such a young child become possessed? Rose wondered. Rose needed to talk to someone who could explain some things to her, and fast. But who? She thought for a moment, then decided to call Deborah. Maybe, just maybe she would be home, and she lived only a matter of blocks away from the gym. Rose dialed her number. "Deborah, I'm at the gym and something is very wrong. I can't explain it over the telephone, but I have got to see you. If something doesn't happen soon I am going to lose it completely. Satan just showed himself to me through a small child here at the health club."

"Give me about thirty minutes to comb my hair and get dressed and I'll be right there." She didn't hesitate for one moment when Rose told her she needed her.

Rose closed her eyes and said a quiet prayer, "Thank you." She stayed on the inside of the gym looking out the window for Deborah. When Deborah's little car finally did drive up, Rose ran out the door of the gym and jumped into the car almost before Deborah could come to a complete stop. Rose knew she was a little over anxious to say the least, and she realized that to the average onlooker, she probably even appeared to be a mad woman at this point, but she couldn't help herself. Her mind was so stressed, so anxious, and she knew she could not possibly take one more thing. Not one. She *was* being driven mad. She broke down and wept as she explained to Deborah about the mystery child in the gym. "I just don't know how much longer I can go on this way," she lamented.

At Deborah's home, the two women marched past Deborah's husband in the garage and went straight to the living room. Deborah tried to make Rose feel relaxed and comfortable. She offered Rose a soft drink, which Rose gladly accepted. Rose was so anxious that she puffed on a few cigarettes, even though she had just worked out.

Deborah could sense Rose's desperation. "In a few minutes, Rose, I am going to come over and put my hands on your head, and I am going to pray for you. I am going to ask the Lord to relieve the pressure you are feeling. Satan has been tormenting you by putting fear in you, and you need to be relieved of the pressure it has put on your mind. But, I'll have to wait until I feel the Holy Spirit move me before I can do that."

The Ancient Paths

They sat in silence for a few moments; then as Rose looked up at Deborah again, she saw a light around her, like the light she had seen on Jeff at his home. "Are you ready now?" Rose asked her.

Deborah nodded her head. She got up off the couch and walked over behind the chair in which Rose was sitting. Rose didn't think she had ever had anyone lay hands on her before. She had heard of it, but she wasn't sure what to expect, if anything. Deborah placed her hands on Rose's head and began to pray. "Heavenly Father, we ask to come before your throne, and ask you to please step in and stop this fear that Satan has been putting in Rose. Lord, we lift her up to you in prayer and ask you to remove the fear and the pressure that have been put in her mind and on her heart. In Jesus Name, Amen."

Rose's eyes were closed while Deborah prayed. Her first thought was, "Nothing's happening." Then Rose prayed silently, "Lord Jesus, if you're real, please come into my heart. If I've blocked you from my heart before, I'm sorry." Then all at once, it was like a volcano exploded in her mind. She was 'seeing' into the spirit realm. Rose could see that she was sitting in a black pit, and all she could think of was how dark it was. Suddenly, it felt as though an invisible hand reached down and lifted her out of that place called darkness. It was done with lightning speed, as she felt layers and layers and layers of darkness--pain, shame, addiction, anger, guilt, loneliness, fear, demonic oppression and bitterness being cast from her. She now knew exactly where she had been, and it was mind boggling. It felt like she had been in hell. It was actually physically painful as she felt herself being yanked out of that pit so quickly and she screamed!

At the same instant in which so much was happening, all at once a pure white, radiant light appeared in the room. It seemed to come from nowhere, and then it fell on Rose. She looked down at her body and there was light so bright and so pure all over her that she could not believe her eyes. She was lit up like a Christmas tree. The light was so bright and pure it was like a refiner's fire in her bones, purging the darkness that had tried for so long to claim her. She didn't have to look at her face in a mirror to know she looked different, she could feel that she was different. She *was* different!

All of this transpired within seconds, and she wondered exactly how long she had been sitting there. Rose broke down and wept, "Oh my God. Oh my God! Oh my God!!" But this time when she cried, it was a cry of relief and joy. She had been lifted out of darkness, out of that hell hole. All her life it seemed she had been crying out for someone to hear her and to understand what she was going through, but now she had found someone who understood—Jesus. She was free, and her chains had been broken. She would never be alone again. This was redemption!

"Honey, if anyone had walked into this room, Christian or non-Christian, they could not have denied the spirit of the Lord was on you. I saw that light." It was true. "I have never seen such purity in my life. The Devil came to kill, steal and destroy, Rose, and he was having a heyday with you. Jesus forgives us, cleanses us, and he sets us free from the curse of sin and death. Now comes the really hard part. It's up to you go forward and forgive. You need to forgive all those who have wronged you, and I realize there have been more than a few, honey. When Peter asked Jesus how often he should forgive his brother who has sinned against him, he asked the Lord if he should forgive his brother seven times. But Jesus replied to Peter, "I say not unto you, until seven times: but, until seventy times seven." Rose, someone once told you to ask for the ancient paths. Today, you have found the ancient path, the good way, now walk in it." And Rose somehow knew for a certainty that beginning today, this day in her life, things would never be the same again.

About the Author

On one side of my family, I am the offspring of a woman that came from the countryside in Tennessee, close to Nashville. That family had a rich heritage and has been in Tennessee for seven generations to the best of my knowledge.

On the other side of my family, was my dad, who remained an enigma until his death. He was a complex individual who brought with him a secret past.

During my childhood, my family moved around quite a bit since my father was in the military. It was difficult for me and my three siblings to put down roots and make lasting friendships as children. But eventually, there were some friendships which would become lasting. While picking up the family and moving around was really a hardship as a child, it would serve me well by helping me to become more discerning as I grew older. At some point, it becomes easier to discern the hearts of those who are close to you and you develop what is commonly referred to as 'street smarts.' As I have aged, I have learned some very difficult lessons--they are not always easy to learn. I had a heart for film, so I studied screenwriting at Watkins Film Institute. From there, I had one semester of a class at Belmont University called 'The Fourth Genre,' which was a reference to the genre known as creative nonfiction. I was fascinated with how memories/memoirs/historical data could combine with creativity and imagination to create a tale based on true events.

Before studying film and eventually obtaining a Liberal Arts degree, I received my certification as an ordained minister. However, even given my love for the arts, I have maintained a regular job working in offices as administrative assistant or office manager for years.

I love writing, and if it is done, it should be done with your whole heart and with passion. So, I hope you will take the lessons which are to be learned from this story, and that some of the imagination that went into creating the tale of "The Ancient Paths" will come through.

The Ancient Paths

© TXu-1-849-675 January 28, 2013

ISBN-13:978-1542352819
ISBN-10:1542352819

Works Cited

1. The New Interpreters Study Bible New Revised Standard Version With The Apocrypha. 2003. Abindgon Press. Nashville, TN 37202.

Heart of My Heart Publishing Co., LLC

www.heartofmyheart.org

Cover photo was found at

https://www.facebook.com/groups/propheticartsforjesus/

Made in the USA
Lexington, KY
20 April 2017